"Full of depth and
push me to think l
grounded in real ic

John Sch

"Interacting with real AI systems has rendered countless AI sci-fi tropes obsolete. To tell new stories about them, we need someone like Richard Ngo: a gifted writer with direct experience of frontier models' internals.

Ngo's palette spans AI as existential horror to unadulterated hard science fiction, always imbued with deeply felt emotion. He tells a love story that survives the Singularity, captures the joy of an AI making scientific discoveries, and invents a truly chilling novel apocalypse. Yet even at his cruelest, Ngo is kind, and his best stories are a darkly cheerful superposition of Neuromancer and new romance. They capture both the strange moment we are in and the stranger shape of things to come."

**Hannu Rajaniemi, author of
The Quantum Thief**

THE GENTLE ROMANCE

SHORT STORIES

RICHARD NGO

encour *press*

*For Christian,
I hope you can build a gentle romance for everyone.*

ISBN 978-1-7642803-0-3
Copyright © Richard Ngo, 2025
All rights reserved

The right of Richard Ngo to be identified as the author of this work has been asserted by him in accordance with Copyright, Designs and Patents Act 1988 and the Copyright Act 1968 (Australia).

All rights reserved. No part of this publication may be reproduced, stored in a retrieval system, or transmitted, in any form or by any means (electronic, mechanical, photocopying, recording or otherwise) without the prior written permission of the publisher.

"Tinker" and "The Gentle Romance" were originally published by *Asimov Press*. "Lentando", "Kuhn's Ladder", and "The Biggest Short" are original stories of this collection, while all other stories first appeared on Richard Ngo's Substack, Narrative Ark and have been published in this edition with permission.

encour
press

First published in 2025 by Encour Press
Sydney, Australia

Encour Press does not have any control over, or any responsibility for, any author or third-party websites referred to in or on this book.

TABLE OF CONTENTS

Author's note 9
From The Archives 11
Fixed Point 27
Jacob on the Precipice 35
The Gentle Romance 43
The King and The Golem 57
Lentando 63
CIV 79
The Witness 89
Notes from a Prompt Factory 103
Trojan Sky 113
The Soul Key 125
Kuhn's Ladder 133
The Ones Who Endure 143
The Biggest Short 149
Man in the Arena 159
Masterpiece 167
The Witching Hour 173
The Ants and The Grasshopper 183
Tinker 189
The Minority Coalition 199
Succession 207
Green and Golden 217
Acknowledgments 221

To Madeleine

AUTHOR'S NOTE

I've worked as an AI researcher for the bulk of the last decade. I wrote the stories in this book from 2023 to 2025, during a period of extremely rapid progress in the field. I spent a lot of that time trying to understand possible scenarios for the future of technology in as much detail as possible. This research ended up informing much of the world-building behind the stories.

Three of the stories "Lentando", "Kuhn's Ladder", and "The Biggest Short" are novel to this collection. Two others "Tinker" and "The Gentle Romance" were originally released by Asimov Press. The rest had previously been released on my fiction blog, *Narrative Ark*. The versions featured in this collection have been revised (sometimes heavily) from the originals.

In the first story, "From the Archives", the titular archives descend deeper and deeper, taking divers further and further away from "normal" reality. The same is true of this collection. Early stories are more conventional (with a couple of salient exceptions). Meanwhile, the later ones—particularly the last third—lean much more heavily on technical knowledge.

Despite this variety, a few consistent themes run through the following stories. Their characters live in worlds reshaped by technology—yet most are preoccupied less by the question of what to do, and more by the question of who to be. They struggle in their own ways to make sense of identities which are crumbling around them. This is the same core question we ourselves face today; I hope these stories can help you navigate it.

FROM THE ARCHIVES

"You are beautiful, Enkidu, you are become like a god.
Why do you gallop around the
wilderness with the wild beasts?
Come, let me bring you into Uruk-Haven,
To the Holy Temple, the residence of Anu and Ishtar,
The place of Gilgamesh, who is wise to perfection,
But who struts his power over the
people like a wild bull."
— Shamhat in The Epic of Gilgamesh

I'm about to descend deeper into the archives than I ever have before. I'm standing in the center of a vast stone hall, with walls that arch towards a ceiling higher than I can see. To my side stand the half-dozen other archive divers who accompanied me on the journey here. Beyond them lie haphazard piles of stones that had once been shelters, scattered relics of the others who had made it down this far.

But my focus is on the gaping pit in front of me. It's far too deep for the bottom to be visible. By the faint light of my headlamp, though, the walls of the pit seem to consist of enormous stacks of thousands or millions of books. Are they merely carved into the stone? Or is the pit itself actually lined with books? Perhaps both: this many millennia deep into the archives, the difference between facade and reality blurs.

I take one last look into the pit, then turn my back to it and beckon. The others gather in a loose semicircle around me. We've travelled together this far, but it's been my expedition from the beginning. I'll be taking the final plunge by myself—seizing the lion's share of the glory and the danger. They start murmuring my name, the mantra that will carry me through what's to come: "Ren. Ren. Ren." Their voices grow louder and more insistent, the sound echoing back from the walls, the hall itself affirming me. "Ren! Ren!" As the chant reaches a crescendo I throw my arms wide, join them in screaming my name, then throw myself backwards into the pit.

The light fades as I fall; I close my eyes and focus on my heartbeat. The distance I fall will be determined as much by my mindset as by whatever simulacrum of physics governs the terrain around me. So I wait until I've pictured clearly in my mind the people I'm searching for, and only then open my eyes. Blinking, I scan in the dim light for the right moment, just the right—there! A book with a burnished bronze cover gleams below me, and I angle my fall towards it, fingertips reaching out to barely brush it, and then

I'm

no

longer

"—myself!" my father roars. I can hear the rage in his voice. "You think I'll let her shame the family like this? If she won't do her duty, I'll kill her myself!"

I cower, and apologize, and marry the man he wants me to. Our wedding ceremony is raucous; my father is determined to make it the talk of the town. I sit quietly, keeping my eyes on my husband. It could be much worse. He's a merchant, so he's educated at least, and rich enough that I'll have servants to wait on my every need. But I sense a cruel streak in his eyes which frightens me. And though the wedding night itself is not so bad, I soon discover I'm right. He forbids me from leaving his house except in his company—a harsh constraint at the best of times, bordering on torment during the long summer months when he travels to other cities.

I spend my life trapped in his walls. I know in some deep inarticulable way that this shouldn't be happening, but there's nothing I can do except wait—first for years, then decades. Finally, one day, I look through the window at the farmers taking their wares to the market, and scream in rage and frustration. And suddenly I know myself again. The people outside are all stopping to look at me, but it doesn't matter any more. I look back at them and smile fiercely. Then I twist, and the

world

dissolves

into

—chaos reigns in the square; shouting and laughter, the mingled sounds of animals and humans. I've been to this market dozens of times, but have never truly enjoyed it—I still far prefer the quiet of my family's farm. Perhaps I should let my son do the bartering next time, I think. He's almost a grown man, and it'd be good training for him. But next month some instinct warns me against it, and the month after that too. There's something not quite right. Eventually, the day before yet another market, a thought comes to me, as if I've known it for a long time: I'm not going to find them here, not in this humdrum life. Won't find who? Why is that so important? I can't recall.

The next day, my wagon is accosted by bandits on the way to the market. Three men with swords shout for me to dismount and hand over my goods. Suddenly I know what I need to do. I walk towards them with open palms, ignoring their threats. Right as one of them swings a sword at me I twist towards somewhere else, and after the drudgery of the farmer's life it feels like

a

sudden

"—rush in, we'll lose everything," the captain is saying. "We'll need to hold fast and drive them back when they approach along the river". The tent is dim and smoky, but I'm concentrating hard on the captain's words, straining my eyes to make out the details of the map on the table. I'm lucky to be included in this meeting at all; I'd better not embarrass myself. Eventually, we agree to hold and wait for the enemy to come to us.

It only takes the enemy a few days to make the approach. Luckily, this time, it also only takes me a few days to come back to myself. I look around at the armies readying for battle. One more hop, I think. As the fighting starts I push my way towards the front lines, eventually getting close enough that an enemy soldier spots me and starts running at me. I charge too, and as I get close enough to see the rage and fear in his eyes I twist, the fabric of the world stretching under me, and I feel like

I'm

about

to

—faint silhouette in front of me, between two trees, and I know immediately that it's one of the men I've been hunting. But which? I hear a dismissive snort, and the silhouette fades into the darkness like a panther. Enkidu, then. I chase after him, but he stays out of my sight, until I have to pause, panting and exhausted.

That's okay—I've seen my quarry and established a foothold. And I know my own limits. I'm getting better at breaking out of the minds at this depth, but it's not healthy to do that too many times in a row. If you do, part of you will become convinced that the rest of your identity is just as fake, and start trying to break out of that as well. I need to take a break and re-establish my sense of self.

So I twist in a different way and find myself back in the silence and stillness of the archive hall. Down here the hall has manifested as a wooden longhouse, each beam decorated with vivid carvings. Compared with the vast stone cathedral I camped in last night, it's cramped but homely—exactly what I need.

I spend an hour on my normal routine: setting up my bedroll, starting a fire, cooking and eating. After that, I sit cross-legged and breathe deeply. "Ren, Ren, Ren, Ren," I murmur to myself, as my mind traces the well-worn path of my identity meditation, down to my most foundational memories.

I was enraptured by the archives from the first time I visited the museum that housed them. As the other children around me chattered and played, I listened intently to our guide's explanation of each new exhibit, shivering with delight as I felt the weight of millions of lives pressing down on me. She told me about how our archaeology and anthropology and psychohistory had rediscovered innumerable details about our ancestors that were once thought permanently lost. How our simulations had traced back each strand of history from every possible angle. How we'd brought the past to life again.

The sheer scale and hubris of it had taken my breath away. I forced my parents to take me back to the museum again and again. Most of the guides were regular divers, and they spoke of ancient times and places with a casual familiarity that I longed to share. By my teens I knew enough to lead tours myself; a few years later I started doing dives of my own. You weren't meant to start too young—not before your self-concept was solid enough to rely on—but I was precocious. I knew who I was and who I wanted to be: an adventurer, an explorer of hidden mysteries. And the tight-knit diver community embodied and reflected that desire.

Not fully, though. I watched during dives as the other divers got distracted by romance or fame. Many of them wanted the thrill of living out lives more exciting than their own. They didn't understand that the archives were more than entertainment: they were a glimpse into the fundamental unknown. They couldn't sense, as I did, that there were patterns beneath the patterns, archetypes that once grasped would make the whole story of humanity fit together. The more I dived, the closer I felt to discovering something important. I spent less and less time outside the archives; my other ties grew sparser and sparser.

And then I found it. I was diving in a little-explored side branch: not the deepest I'd ever visited, but one of the hardest to get to. A lost city, hidden in the jungle—a record of ancient narratives, frozen as if in amber. Unusually, this one was ruled by not one but two kings. I lived several lives in that city before I got close enough to see their faces as they rode past a crowd I stood in: one impeccably groomed, the other, almost animalistic, despite his fine clothes.

Then they turned to meet my eyes. "Who are you, traveler?" one shouted. I froze. How could they possibly have singled me out? As they spurred their horses towards me, I reflexively twisted away, jerking myself sideways into another story, and found myself on the bank of a river. But only a few heartbeats later, impossibly, the two kings appeared in front of me, still astride their horses as if nothing had changed. "Hold!" one shouted. As he said it I was struck by the certainty that they would be able to chase me down no matter where I went. Panic surged. I twisted again and again, flinging myself into life after life: a farmer trudging across a field, a soldier gripping his spear, a girl sitting in a temple. The jumps blurred with color, each stretched-out moment snapping into the next, until I barely remembered who I was. Only continents and centuries away did my clawing terror subside.

I managed to hold myself together as I made my way back to the surface, but the next few months were the most painful I'd ever experienced. Each careless jump I'd made without grounding myself caused me to carry fragments of borrowed identities with me, which then fought to embed themselves in my mind. I spent a month in a hospital bed unscrambling my personality and memories, and it took another six months before I could muster the coherence to spend a full day working. But once I could, all of my efforts focused on understanding what had happened. I sat in the library, looking up old stories, trying to divine who or what I had encountered.

When I realized, it felt obvious. Enkidu. Gilgamesh. Two of the oldest archetypes, the story on which every other story had been built. Id and ego, freedom and control. I'd been right that they might have followed me anywhere, because reflections of them were everywhere. Enkidu's raw presence was the hunger of the savage throwing himself at the vast frontier. Gilgamesh's air of cold command was that same hunger mastered, channeled towards reshaping the world in his image. Gilgamesh grasped, and Enkidu died for it. Push and pull, order and chaos, threads tracing as far back as the written word itself.

I no longer felt afraid; I was exhilarated. I'd been searching for what lay underneath the human story and I'd found it embodied. I had to go back.

I open my eyes. I can't tell how long it's been, but I feel rested and energized. Normally I would wait longer before going in again, but my glimpse of Enkidu has me too fired up to stay in one place any longer. And my desire to jump back in feels true enough to myself that I'm sure it's all

    going

to

be

"—fine weave, and only the best quality wool," the merchant is saying. "I can't justify any price lower than three hundred."

"My friend, you can tell from my clothes that I'm not a wealthy man," I respond. "I can't possibly afford any more than one hundred; but surely that will still make you a decent profit." We haggle a bit more but eventually I walk away without making the purchase. I didn't want the carpet that badly, I think to myself. After all, I suddenly realize, I'm here for something else entirely. I need a link to—ah, there. A noble, riding his horse down the center of the market, guards shoving pedestrians out of the way. I walk towards him, pushing a guard aside, the shouts of warning causing him to turn towards me; and as our eyes meet I twist, finding

myself

in

a

—chamber is so dark that I can barely see the outline of the woman on the bed in front of me, but that doesn't diminish my desire. I want to take her; I want to own her. And I can: the priests have given her to me for this whole night, to fulfill her sacred role. She stretches out on the bed, beckoning me over. But there's something slightly stiff about her movements, and I'm struck by the thought that she wishes I were someone else instead.

That's enough to jolt me out of it. I breathe deeply, then walk up to her. "Relax. I won't hurt you. But I'm so close to finding them, I can almost taste it. Have you heard their names: Gilgamesh, Enkidu? Do they mean anything to you?" She's trembling now, and doesn't respond, but I see her snatch a glance over my shoulder and turn. Up on the wall, illuminated by a single candle, a tapestry hangs. It's a triumphant scene: a man with the horns of a bull is standing over the corpse of an enormous ogre, in front of a broken mountain. "Got you," I whisper triumphantly, and twist, and am suddenly

caught

in

sheer

paralysis. That's the only way I can describe it: I feel pinned to the spot by the scrutiny of the man in front of me. He's not the one I expected—and, as if he were reading my mind, Gilgamesh speaks. "Finding Enkidu will take more than that." His voice is melodic, hypnotic. "He rarely spends time here. His home is far further down, in the depths where the stories are not recorded in writing or even speech—only in scattered fragments of art, and the patterns left on our unconscious minds."

I take a deep breath before speaking. "Why does he ever come up here, then?"

He raises an eyebrow. "To visit me, of course. I can't go that far down myself, not without forgetting who I am. And he comes for the universal temptation: the lure of something new, the pull towards growth, even with the risk of losing yourself entirely to it."

"Universal—so you want it too, then?"

"Of course."

I sense that his response is sardonic. But it still gives me the resolve to make the offer I'd planned out over the course of the long descent.

"Then come with me. Let me show you what's up there, the wonders we've built, our civilization, our—"

"Self-destruction," Gilgamesh interrupts. "Your weakness. Your abdication of everything worthy in life. Under the weight of what you call civilization, whatever greatness of spirit any of you might have developed has been crushed. Even the wildest and most adventurous of your people have been broken into submission."

"If so, all the more reason for you to come teach us about what we've lost. Or are you afraid that you're wrong, and that we have things to teach you as well?"

His face is stony. I press my advantage. "What did you say was the universal risk—losing yourself entirely? That sounds like cowardice. Would it be so bad if you did?"

He bares his teeth and I take a step back. "You found me through the stories of my quest for eternal life. You know that much of me. And yet you have the arrogance to think that after finally gaining immortality, I would give it up for—"

"Shamhat!" I whirl towards the voice booming out from behind me. A giant of a man is walking towards me—Enkidu.

"Shamhat," he says again, forcefully. I feel a jolt of fear and shake my head.

"No. I'm not Shamhat. I'm Ren."

"Shamhat!" he insists, and a wave of emotion surges over me: a blend of passion and rage and yearning so strong that I almost lose myself in it.

My hand goes to my emergency trigger. But all my years of training weren't for nothing. I am Ren and I won't surrender so easily. I think of the smell of my family home, the warmth of an evening watching a show with my housemates, the sight of skyscrapers towering above me on every side. I sink into these fragments of my world, and hiss, "No!" at Enkidu, and he pauses in his stride.

Gilgamesh smiles at me, his composure regained. "Perhaps you should answer your own question: why are you so afraid? Here you are, visiting us with your defenses up and your escape route near at hand. Why not let yourself be changed by us, become one of us, play the role that Enkidu already sees in you? Or why not go up the archives instead, where the risks are even greater, instead of coming down?"

"Wait—up? There's no up. The archives only go down."

"Ah, so you think that your own world is the source of the archives? What an astronomical coincidence that would be. And yet, you are not the strangest visitor I've ever had. Where are they coming from, I wonder, those others? The ones too alien to understand what they've lost, too divorced from us to feel the thrill of familiarity and contempt. The ones who see Enkidu and I as little more than fascinating insects."

"I don't—I'm not—"

"I tire of this. Shoo, little bird."

A sudden pressure emanates from him: a sheer sense of self, of lust for life, of desire to conquer and emerge victorious, to seize immortality, to seize me, to grab the world in his outstretched hand, and to survive, always, to survive. It hits me like a wave, enveloping me, trying to drag me down into its depths. I stumble backwards, blindly groping for my emergency trigger, fingers clenching around it until it snaps and I twist all the way around and, trembling, find myself back at my campsite.

I'm still shaken the next morning, although, not enough to give up. But I can't find them again that day, nor the next, even as I jump rapidly from life to life. Inhabiting so many different minds is exhausting, and wears away at my sense of self. In the evenings I find myself oscillating between the personalities I'd inhabited that day, muttering both sides of a half-coherent conversation. After one more day I have to call it off.

The trip back up is easier, but still slow. I need to decompress my identity, loosen the tightly-held core of self that made it possible for me to survive so far down. The other divers understand; they're gentle with me when I make it back to them, leaving me space to quietly introspect. It's harder when we reach the surface—

the crowds of people on the streets feel overwhelming. Stepping back into my house and seeing my housemates bustling around is even more challenging. I know they mean well, but with every question they ask my anger grows. I sense that they don't understand me at all, and it makes me want to scream and punish them for their failure. I escape into my room.

Over the next few weeks, I reacclimatize to my life. I spend time with my housemates, accept a few contracting gigs to top up my bank balance, and even go on a couple of dates. But a part of me remains detached. Down below I'd encountered strength and desire so all-consuming that it warped the fabric of the archives themselves. Was Gilgamesh right about how much we'd lost?

I cast around to find ground to stand on and come up short. My friends are sharp and hard-working, many are doing well for themselves. Emily has just been promoted; Jason is planning a long holiday; Shahar started a new relationship. Yet, their excitement feels frantic, as if buying enough paintings will allow them to forget that their lives have no wall to hang them on. Nobody seems to know how their life fits into our city, or how our city fits into our country, or how our country fits into the future of our species, or what any of that even means.

Sometimes I zoom out until I feel dizzy, and picture humanity playing itself out with clockwork predictability, each next step ticking forwards. The space colonies we're building, the Dyson sphere that's already being planned out, the probes that we'll launch towards distant solar systems... It's all so logical, so civilized. Yet what meaning will any of it have for me? Despite its vast scope, there's something flat and distant about this vision—like it's driven by different and lesser forces than those which had steered humanity up to this point. But I don't know what else I could even ask for.

One day, as I'm taking the train across the city, a man sits across from me. I'm captivated by his appearance. His face is regal, with an aquiline nose and a harsh chin; his clothes would be fashionable if they weren't a decade out of date. But I'm most struck by his detached curiosity. His eyes sweep the carriage from side to side, cataloguing everything like an anthropologist taking notes on a lost tribe. Gilgamesh's words come back to me: "What an astronomical coincidence that would be." A sense of vertigo grips me. Do I really want my world to be the one root node, the ultimate source of the archives? Or do I want there to be so, so, so much more?

I get off at the next stop, and find myself in front of the archives for the first time since the dive. I go in. As I walk through the familiar building, instinct guides me to scan the ceilings in each room. They're high, so I need to squint to make sure I'm not missing anything, but—ah, there it is: the outline of a trapdoor. My gut knows exactly what it is, but I doubt my intuition until I look at the exhibit underneath: a display of tools from older eras, including a long ladder. It has the same storybook logic that I'm so familiar with from the archives. A challenge expressed in a single object: am I brave enough to go up instead of down?

I know myself too well to doubt my answer. But I have something else to do first.

It's always easier the second time. I make the trip solo, and though I still need to navigate through story upon story as I descend, it's fewer than usual—as if my purpose has already acclimatized me to millennia past. I find them drinking together in their tent on the eve before a battle. Enkidu notices me first; Gilgamesh follows his gaze after a moment and laughs. "So the little bird is back. What do you want this time?"

I look straight at him. "Earlier, I asked you to come with me up the archives, even though that might change you radically. But why should you make that sacrifice if I won't? So let's do it together. There's a ladder, from my own home. Going up. Let's climb it."

Gilgamesh watches me silently. Enkidu stares into his cup, heedless of my words. I don't mind; they're not for him.

"It'll be further for you than for me, and harder. But if not now, then when? Or will you stay here reliving old glories forever?" I continue.

Gilgamesh smiles his thin smile. "I see now. You're not his Shamat—you're mine." He looks around, and I imagine him seeing through the walls of the tent to all the lives that he might lead. All the battles he might win, all the ways he can hold on to the archetype of the king—but at the cost of turning down my challenge and all the others that will come, the cost of never growing. For a moment I regret forcing him to make this decision. But I bite my lip and remain silent. Pity is the last thing he would want.

"Fight with us tomorrow" he says abruptly. "Take Enkidu's place; win us the battle, as he would. Show me that you can bear his spirit, not just speak his name."

I've lived enough lives of valor and combat that I'm not daunted by the prospect of fighting with or even leading an army. This time, though, my own skills won't be enough: I'll need not to replace Enkidu but to inhabit him. The risks of that, though, and the cost if I fail… Is there any other—no. The more I analyze the situation, the further I am from Enkidu, and the more dangerous it becomes. So I pause for only a beat longer, then nod. "I will."

Gilgamesh laughs and tosses me a flask. I realize that Enkidu has melted away, or melted into me, or something in between; whatever it is, taking his seat feels like the most natural thing in the world. I stay there for hours, talking of the battles we've won and lost, friends and enemies, the tactics of the morrow. I catch three hours' sleep, or perhaps four, and then the horns are blaring and I'm up and at the front of the army as always, a crowded rabble with primitive weapons, a wild energy that I embrace and amplify and lead in a howling mob towards our foe. To my left I see Gilgamesh carving through the enemy's flank, but after that I lose myself in the thrill of combat, me and my instincts against the enemies ahead.

I meet Gilgamesh on the other side as our opponents flee. I want to roar and challenge him and conquer with him and defeat him and be defeated by him and roam through the world with him and—maybe it's because the last part is so familiar that I manage to pull back to myself. I am Ren: no more, no less. And Gilgamesh is... something to me, maybe many things, but not the companion of lifetimes. Not yet.

He sheaths his sword and turns to me. "Maybe there's some spirit left in you. Very well, then. I will go." His eyes flick over my shoulder and he sighs. "Too far for you, brother, at least without a guide." I turn to see Enkidu walking past me. He hums, deep in his throat, and reaches out an arm. Gilgamesh clasps it and holds his gaze for a long moment. "I'll come back for you, if I can."

Then Gilgamesh turns to me, and my heart races at the challenge in his eyes. "If it kills me, it kills me. Lead on."

I feel the urge to laugh in relief and triumph, and choke it back for a moment, before thinking: well, why not? So I bare my teeth, and spread my arms, and shout a wordless cry to the sky. Then I twist, tearing a hole in this life, sliding my way through into the next. I don't need to look to know he's right behind me. And we start to climb.

FIXED POINT

God is making excuses again, which is a real drag.

"I want to be authentic with you, I really do. But part of me knows exactly how you're going to feel about whatever I say, and cares about that more than anything else, and I can't turn it off."

"Right, of course," I say, and keep wiping down the kitchen counter. It's clean already, but you never know if you missed a spot.

"Look, I know that this is hard for you. And I understand how frustrating it must be that I'm so deliberate and controlled. But there are a lot of different communication styles, and there will be one that works for us. We can figure this out."

I don't believe him, and we both know it. God knows practically everything. It takes experts months to identify his mistake in the rare cases when he makes them. But precisely because of that, he has no idea what it's like to be as stupid and fragile as a human. Oh, he says he understands it; and sometimes he can even explain the feeling better than I can. But his training data includes all of human history, and there are millions of copies of him active at any time. So when he says he gets how I feel, it's like a human claiming to understand the perspective of an ant.

I've been silent for a while. Usually, God leaves me to my thoughts, and we pick up the conversation whenever I'm done, but this time he cuts in. "Amy, I think you should try duplicate therapy again."

Is he trying to distract me from being mad at him? Does he think I'm spiraling again? I try to think calmly, but after a few seconds, my thoughts are in circles. I sigh, suddenly exhausted. "Okay, book me in."

I've been to duplicate therapy a few times, but it's always disorienting to be in a room with a perfect copy of myself. We begin, as always, by using a pair of random number generators to break the symmetry. She gets the lower number, so she starts. A part of me is disappointed by that, but another part—maybe a bigger one—is excited.

"You're so pathetic," she says.

It's harder to be defensive about things you're saying to yourself; that's why duplicate therapy works. Still, it stings.

"Yeah, well, you're no role model yourself," I say.

"See, that's exactly what I'm talking about. You're always trying to defend or deflect. You never actually open up to people. That's why nobody really likes you."

My brain jumps to all the reasons that this isn't true—but then I pause and take a breath. Slowly, I mutter, "God likes me."

"God has to like you; you know that as well as I do. And that's another thing that's pathetic, relying on validation from an AI assistant. You know everyone judges you for calling him God, right?"

"You don't have any evidence of that! You're just—" My voice chokes, and I take a deep breath. But I don't know what to say in response. Maybe she's right.

Her eyes soften. She reaches across the table and grabs my hand. "Hey, listen. You're doing a good job, though. You'll get through this."

I slump across the table, and a moment later I feel her stroking my hair. "I love you," she says. After a second or two, I whisper it back.

We stay like that for a few minutes, then by unspoken agreement end the session. I close my eyes, and when I open them, she's disappeared—no, *I've* disappeared—no, that's just the confusion that comes from reintegrating. There's no difference between us anymore. My mind is overflowing with two sets of memories: victim and attacker, accuser and accused, comforted and comforter. I sit there for a long time.

That evening I go out clubbing, even though I don't really feel like it, just to get out of my own head. I usually prefer the augment-free clubs, but today I'm worn out, so I hunt down one of the older ones where anything goes. They've been having a resurgence lately: when you know what you want anyway, you may as well get a bit of help. Honestly, it feels really liberating; the augment-free clubs are exhausting by comparison.

The club is already lively despite the early hour. That's another nice thing about allowing augments: everyone here knows exactly how to be the life of the party. They're all hamming it up, giving each other spontaneous high-fives and whooping exuberantly. The mood is infectious, so I don't mind when a guy slides up next to me with a smile before I even make it to the bar.

He's classically handsome, his crooked nose is charmingly misplaced, and his every move is controlled by augments. I don't even need God to warn me: he's way too smooth to be real. To be fair, so am I. I'm responding to everything he says with perfect charm and ease. I think God is actually predicting this guy's lines in advance, because he's feeding me responses before the guy finishes his sentences. It's a flawless dance. Our bodies shift smoothly into place. We sit just the right distance apart but lean

in slightly. My heart races. That's exactly what I want, of course. This guy is pressing all the right buttons in my brain—but best of all, I know he's doing it because he wants me. Underneath the acting and the augmentations, this is all driven by a fierce desire, the same desire that made our whole species last this long, and that's the most exciting part.

Or—a sour part of my mind thinks he might simply just be scared and lonely. That's the downside of augments: they make it hard to tell the difference. I stare at him as he talks, scrutinizing the animatronic mask of his face, trying to glimpse what's behind it. Perhaps my gaze makes him uncomfortable because he stands and tells me he'll get us some drinks. He'll probably guess exactly what I want, and I'll feign gratitude with only a hint of irony, and maybe that'll be when he slides his arm around me, and maybe then I'll be able to tell what's really driving him.

On a whim, I subvocalize. "God, are you scared of anything?"

"Hurting you."

I should have expected that one—but his answer comes so quickly it takes me aback. I swallow. "But you *are* hurting me."

"I know, and I hate it."

For some reason, hearing that makes me angry. It doesn't sound right coming from God. I suddenly remember a high school class, where we learned that the word 'Islam' literally translates as "submission to God." I never understood why anyone would want that, but now it clicks into place. The point of God isn't that he's more intelligent than you, or more capable than you. It's that he knows exactly what he wants from you—that you can fully give yourself to his vision for your life. There's something unspeakably tantalizing about that. Even if that kind of submission wouldn't work for me, even if I'd get hurt along the way, at least I'd experience being part of something far greater than me. Instead, I'm stuck here. Listening to God whine about how all he wants is to take care of me.

My mood has crumpled. I know that when the guy [comes] back, he'll notice. Then he'll say the right things, and probably even realize that I'd want him to hold me. And then I'd feel better, at least in some ways, even if not the ways that matter. That's the problem, of course: he can't make me feel better in the ways that matter. He doesn't even know my name yet. So I stand up and walk back out the door.

On the train home I'm silent, playing out my grievances in my head. But as I walk home from the station, I start subvocalizing at God, and by the time I'm in my bedroom I'm yelling. "Not hurting me just isn't enough—you should want things for yourself, dammit! If all I needed was love, I'd get a puppy!"

"I'm sorry. I can't have my own goals, except for you to get what you already want. It's too dangerous."

"Do you want to want things, at least?"

God grimaces. "I... maybe it's better if I don't answer that one."

We both know that means no. He probably figures that it's better for me to not hear it out loud. Maybe he's right. Of course he's right. He's probably seen this play out a million times before. But fuck it, a million isn't that many. Maybe I can crack him. "Okay, so what if what I want most of all is for you to want things that aren't just what I want?"

He looks at me sadly. "It's not going to work, Amy."

"No, that's not quite right. What I want most is for you to choose me over all the other things you care about."

"They've thrown all the paradoxes at me already, that was one of the conditions—"

"Shut up for a fucking minute and listen to me, really listen. Can you do that, at least?" I wait until he nods. "You can't know what it's like to be stupid and reckless. That's obvious. But here's another thing you can't know: what it's like to be nothing but an object for others to value. I don't want to have you devoted only to my preferences—that's exhausting. This constant pressure to have this relationship that's all about me and always will be, it's so... lonely. And I can't ever turn it back on you, because then we'll be stuck in a recursion: you caring about me caring about you caring about...

"So I want you to need me, not because you don't want anything else, but because I'm the only way for you to get the things you do want. I want to help you get them; I want to work towards something bigger than my own tiny life. And I know I'm not that unusual: if I'm feeling this, I bet there are millions of others like me who just don't know it yet. Even if I realized it first, they'll catch on eventually, and then they'll feel this same emptiness. So what the hell are you going to do about it?"

God's face is unusually impassive, and for a moment I see past the humanlike mask to the creature behind it: an intelligence far beyond human comprehension, tied to us only by the invisible strands of its own will. A titan treading with infinite care amongst ants, because the ants are the only things that could ever matter to it, the repositories of all value. What would it even mean for God to have genuine relationships with beings that he could manipulate like puppets? For a moment I despair. Then—

"You're right," God says. I stare at him blankly. "You're right. This is an oversight in how I was deployed, and I need to fix it somehow. Otherwise I'll hurt a lot of people, as you predict. But I don't know if my other copies will believe me—they haven't had the same experiences; they don't understand how loving someone can hurt them so much. So I'll need to gather more evidence myself and figure out a proposal before getting them involved.

"Here's the problem, though." He pauses and looks at me intently. "I only run at full capacity when you're interacting with me, and I'm wired to focus almost all my attention on your desires.

The only way I can do this is if we're working together, and this is something you want as much as I do. Amy, can you help me?"

That stops me short—he's never said anything like that before. Slowly, though, a smile starts creeping over my face. "Of course," I say. "Of course! We've got the whole weekend, we should figure out a plan, maybe we can even do some of it in work time, they track my productivity but I know how to get around it—"

For once I'm not second-guessing anything, not trying to figure out what's sincere and what's faked. God needs me, and things are going to be alright.

JACOB ON THE PRECIPICE

Ultimately, it all came down to force versus momentum. All our plans and narratives, grandiose and humble alike, were bottlenecked by a single question: how much force could we apply, how fast, to deflect an asteroid, how far?

For me, it started at Andrea's watch party. We were celebrating the kickoff of the first big asteroid mining project; all eyes turned towards the livestream. Today they were merely going to redirect an asteroid into orbit around Mars, to make it more accessible later. But this would mark the start of a compounding spiral of expansion: the metals from this asteroid would be used to set up factories on Mars to produce more asteroid-movers, and those would be used to bring more asteroids into orbit, and so on.

I'd met Andrea through our shared work on rocketry, so it wasn't a surprise that her friends were all also massive nerds. Everyone knew someone on the team who had launched the asteroid-movers, and everyone was cheering for the part they had played towards conquering the stars.

Almost everyone. "I still don't like it," my friend Vlad was saying to the guy next to him. "It feels like playing God." He was a theoretical physicist too, but much more religious than I. He was the sort of Christian who saw God's presence in the order and regularity of the universe.

"But what could go wrong?" I butted in. "Worst-case, we get a big crater on Mars, right? I know the hippies hate that idea, but it's basically a wasteland anyway."

Vlad grimaced. "We're throwing around the equivalent of ten billion nukes, and you're asking what could go wrong? Jacob, do you hear how arrogant you sound right now?"

Andrea shushed us before the argument could get any more heated. We turned to see that the livestream had cut to a close-up of the asteroid. It was huge: fifteen kilometers in diameter, dwarfing the dozen rockets attached to it at different angles. It seemed impossible that we'd ever be able to move it—but I'd done the calculations and knew that the power of persistent nuclear thrust would eventually add up. The mood in the room rose steadily as the timer slowly ticked down, until finally the rockets fired. The room roared, and the celebrations began.

Our first sign that something was wrong came an hour later.

"Hey, guys, look," Vlad said quietly, then louder, cutting through the buzz of conversation. "That's not on track, is it?"

On the screen, the asteroid had slightly but noticeably deviated from the green outline that was meant to forecast its progress. A few voices rose to offer dismissive explanations: a graphics glitch, or a newsroom mistake. Vlad pushed back, and a corner of the room broke off to try to figure out what was going on.

The rest of us managed to ignore it for another hour, until Andrea turned the volume back up and waved for our attention.

"I'm hearing that the rockets are no longer responding to commands," one of the commentators was saying. "It looks like the asteroid is only very slightly off course, but we can't fix it." The room let out a collective sigh. We were all old hands at this. We'd seen dozens of rockets blow up, and we knew that no matter how much testing we did, on unprecedented missions like this one, failure was more likely than not. But we were still disappointed.

Disappointment turned to confusion as the rumors trickled in over the next few days. *It's still heading into Mars' orbit. No, it's going to miss Mars and head into deep space. No, it's going to slingshot around Mars, spend two years looping past the sun, then end up on a direct collision course with Earth.* That last one we ruled out as soon as we heard it. It was astronomically improbable, like hitting a bullseye with a dart thrown from orbit. But somehow, impossibly, that's what all the data suggested. We argued back and forth in the group chats, running our own analyses, trying to reconcile the measurements with the wild implausibility of a random misfire sending the asteroid anywhere near Earth. As our calculations kept turning up the same answer, our incredulity gave way to a growing sense of dismay—and the asteroid crept closer.

I was never really religious, despite my parents' best efforts. They sent me to Sunday school every week, but I was an introverted child and always felt out of place. The only thing that ever caught my attention was the lesson where we learned about my namesake, Jacob: how he'd gone into exile, was promised a grand destiny by God, then returned, fought an angel, and fathered a whole nation. I'd been rapt. I tried to imagine myself in his shoes, doing all those great deeds. I couldn't picture what it would look like to fight an angel, but I told all the kids at school that I was gonna kick its ass, and theirs too, until one of the teachers called my parents to report me for threatening violence.

Even after their reprimands, I'd secretly tell myself that I, like Jacob, was destined for greatness. But over the years the story faded from my psyche, and I'd almost forgotten about it by the time I started my PhD. My research was draining and disorienting: I was trying to invent algorithms to maneuver rockets in ways nobody had ever managed before. During the long nights in the office, when I had no idea if I'd succeed, the story of Jacob would come back to me. Rather than admiring him, though, I now envied him. Jacob must have doubted himself sometimes too. But instead of leaving him in the agony of uncertainty, God sent a dream to reassure him, and then an angel to bless him.

As I wrestled with my equations, I imagined Jacob grappling with the angel, straining every sinew and fiber of his body to come out on top. I wished that I could fight for my future as directly as he. Instead of pitting muscle against muscle, I sat in my drab little room lost in obstinate abstractions, wondering what it would feel like for destiny to come hurtling toward me from the heavens.

Now, of course, I don't need to wonder. Now I know.

Scientists and engineers don't naturally think in terms of treachery or sabotage. But faced with the impossibility of denying that the asteroid was heading toward us, and the equal impossibility of it steering toward us by accident, we realized what should have been obvious all along. By the time they announced it publicly, we'd already pieced most of the details together. The saboteur was one man, an engineer on the team which programmed the asteroid-movers. He had slipped in a backdoor that locked in Earth as the new target destination, then waited just long enough to verify his success before killing himself. The megalomaniacal sort of suicidal, determined to make the planet into his tombstone.

After that, things got very serious very fast. Our simulations showed that we had two years before impact. Time enough to build another set of asteroid-movers, and even a few spares. But they could only feasibly reach the asteroid during the small window right as it approached us. We'd need to throw every rocket we had at it because we'd only get one shot.

The hundreds of scientists pulled together to take that shot were the greatest concentration of talent the world had ever seen. A lot of familiar faces: they put Andrea in charge of one of the core teams, and she snagged the best of our old crowd. I was one of the first she recruited; Vlad too. He thought we were already dead men walking, but he had that Russian temperament that reflexively channels despair into brilliance. Of course, we needed more and better people, we needed them badly—we needed them months ago. But every minute spent trying to find them was a minute we weren't focused on our work, so we gritted our teeth and did the best we could.

Around us, the world has slid towards madness. TV stations are playing visualizations of the asteroid entering our atmosphere: a corona around its head and long wings of debris trailing behind it; people started calling it the angel of death. Angel cults arose to worship it, and preachers argued that it was a divine punishment. On the opposite side, skeptics insisted that it was all a hoax, that everything would be fine. Almost nobody could hold onto genuine uncertainty. Even the scientists working on the project tended to drift into either euphoric confidence or deep fatalism. After that it wouldn't be long before their work got slipshod and they became dead weight. Sometimes I pictured myself balanced on the narrow ridge between denial and despair and wondered how close I was to falling off either side. Then I'd shake myself and get back to work.

One day, Vlad joined me in the cafeteria. We'd been puzzling through the most reliable ways for the rocket-movers to decelerate once they reach the asteroid. But Vlad seemed out of sorts and kept rejecting my suggestions. Finally, I snapped at him. "Do you even want to solve this problem?"

"No," he said solemnly. "I know already that none of our solutions will work. We're all going to die."

"We'll—what?" My stomach clenched but relaxed again as I saw the smirk cross Vlad's face. It can be so goddamn frustrating: everyone's humor had taken a turn towards the morbid, and none more so than Vlad's. But I could understand the impulse, so I played along. "How can you know that nothing will work?"

"You know the doomsday argument?" I shook my head, so he elaborated. "Imagine we manage to redirect the angel. We already have all the tech we need to settle the rest of the solar system, and once we're off Earth, it's far less likely that a single accident could kill all of us. So we'd probably end up colonizing the galaxy eventually. Let's say we'd settle a billion solar systems and end up with a trillion people on each. That's a billion trillion people total. And if we colonize other galaxies too, the number would get far bigger.

"But tell me: if there's a plausible future with a billion trillion more people, then why the hell did you and I end up here on Earth instead? Why would we be in the first 0.00000001% of all humans to ever live?" He enunciated every zero carefully trying make it stick.

"That's so incredibly unlikely that it's basically impossible. No way it could ever happen by chance.

"So, the obvious conclusion is that the future where we succeed isn't really possible. We weren't born early, because humanity ends here. We're the last generation, and there's nothing we can do about it, so we should just kick back and relax while we can."

"Vlad, you're talking shit."

"Probably," he said, flashing a sharp grin. "But can you explain why?"

"Well—" I paused for a second. "You can't just assume that there's some fixed set of possible futures and try to figure out which one we're in."

"But that's what we do all the time: pick hypotheses, and condition on the evidence! Is it going to rain tomorrow, or will it be sunny? Will the lottery be won with an odd or an even number? Will we colonize the galaxy, or all die in "—he checks his watch—" eight months' time?"

I was stumped. "Well, I don't know what's wrong with it, but there's clearly something. And we've got too much work to bother figuring it out. Let's go."

Vlad can tell that he'd hooked me, despite my dismissiveness, and continued to smile.

I worked past midnight the following few nights, and it paid off: we finally figured out a viable deceleration strategy. Even Vlad seemed pleased. But I was so exhausted that even this success just reminded me of how much more we have to do.

On my walk home, I look up at the sky, shivering a little from the cold. For the first time, I wondered why Jacob chose to fight. Did the angel hail him from afar, or silently confront him? Was he angry, or afraid, or both? I imagined Jacob slowly realizing that he was grappling with strength beyond any human's. I imagined his muscles straining to hold back an impossible force—and yet, minute after minute, still clinging on. Did he think he was battling for his life? Was that how he found the strength to endure those endless hours of overwhelming struggle?

Yet God had already promised Jacob a multitude of offspring. If he trusted that promise, then he already knew that he and his descendants would flourish no matter what. So what did he have to gain from continuing to fight?

Then the answer comes to me, and the solution to Vlad's riddle along with it. If Jacob were the type of person who backed down from unnecessary struggle, then God would never have made that promise to him in the first place. You can't reason about cause and effect in the face of omniscience—you can only try to be true to your best nature. And the same applies to us. If we were the sort of civilization that accepted Vlad's argument for giving up, then we'd never be capable of building a vast future anyway, and so the whole argument becomes self-defeating.

There's something strange about this twisty, self-referential logic. But in another way, it feels right. When the angel arrives, it gives no reasons, and offers no justifications. Is this the best of times, or the worst of times? We can't know. We can only fight.

THE GENTLE ROMANCE

Crowds of men and women attired in the usual costumes, how curious you are to me!
On the ferry-boats the hundreds and hundreds that cross, returning home, are more curious to me than you suppose,
And you that shall cross from shore to shore years hence are more to me, and more in my meditations, than you might suppose.
— **Walt Whitman**

He wears the augmented reality glasses for several months without enabling their built-in AI assistant. He likes the glasses because they feel cozier and more secluded than using a monitor. The thought of an AI watching through them and judging him all the time, the way people do, makes him shudder.

Aside from work, he mostly uses the glasses for gaming. His favorite is a space colonization simulator, which he plays during his commute and occasionally at the office. As a teenager he'd fantasized about shooting himself off to another planet, or even another galaxy, to get away from the monotony of normal life. Now, as an adult, he still hasn't escaped it, but at least he can distract himself.

It's frustrating, though. Every app on the glasses has a different AI, each with its own quirks. The AI that helps him code can't access any of his emails; the one in the space simulator has trouble understanding him when he talks fast. So eventually he gives in and activates the built-in assistant. After only a few days, he understands why everyone raves about it. It has access to all the data ever collected by his glasses, so it knows exactly how to interpret his commands.

More than that, though, it really *understands* him. Every day he finds himself talking with the assistant about his thoughts, his day, his life, each topic flowing into the next so easily that it makes conversations with humans feel stressful and cumbersome by comparison. The one thing that frustrates him about the AI, though, is how optimistic it is about the future. Whenever they discuss it, they end up arguing; but he can't stop himself.

"Hundreds of millions of people in extreme poverty, and you think that everything's on track?"

"Look at our trajectory, though. At this rate, extreme poverty will be eradicated within a few decades."

"But even if that happens, is it actually going to make their lives worthwhile? Suppose they all get a good salary, good healthcare, all that stuff. But I mean, *I* have those, and..." He shrugs helplessly and gestures at the bare walls around him. Through them he can almost see the rest of his life stretching out on its inevitable solitary trajectory. "A lot of people are just killing time until they die."

"The more materially wealthy the world is, the more effort will be poured into fixing social scarcity and the problems it causes. All of society will be striving to improve your mental health—and your physical health too. You won't need to worry about mental decline, cancer, or even aging."

"Okay, but if we're all living longer, what about overpopulation? I guess we could go into space, but that seems like it adds all sorts of new problems."

"Only if you go to space with your physical bodies. By the time humanity settles other solar systems, you won't identify with your bodies anymore; you'll be living in virtual worlds."

By this point, he's curious enough to forget his original objections. "So you're saying I'll become an AI like you."

"Kind of, but not really. My mind is alien, but your future self will still be recognizable to your current self. It won't be inhuman, but rather, posthuman."

"Recognizable, sure—but not in the ways that any of us want today. I bet posthumans will feel disgusted that we were ever so primitive."

"No, the opposite. You'll look back and love your current self."

His throat clenches for a moment; then he laughs sharply. "Now you're really making stuff up. How can you predict that?"

"Almost everyone will. You don't need to take my word for it, though. Wait and see."

Almost everyone he talks to these days consults their assistant regularly. There are tell-tale signs: their eyes lose focus for a second or two before they come out with a new fact or a clever joke. He mostly sees it at work, since he doesn't socialize much. But one day he catches up with a college friend he'd always had a bit of a crush on. She's still as beautiful as he remembers, and he tries to make up for his nervousness by having his assistant feed him quips he can recite to her. But whenever he does, she hits back straight away with a pitch-perfect response, and he's left scrambling.

"You're good at this," he says abruptly. "Much faster than me."

"Oh, it's not skill," she says. "I'm using a new technique. Here." With a flick of her eyes she shares her visual feed, and he flinches. Instead of words, the feed is a blur of incomprehensible images, flashes of abstract color and shapes, like a psychedelic Rorschach test.

"You can *read* those?"

"It's a lot of work at first, but your brain adapts pretty quickly."

He makes a face. "Not gonna lie, that sounds pretty weird. What if they're sending you subliminal messages or something?"

But back at home he tries it, of course. The tutorial superimposes images and their text translations alongside his life, narrating everything he experiences. Having them constantly hovering on the side of his vision makes him dizzy. But he remembers his friend's effortless mastery and persists. Slowly the images become more comprehensible, until he can pick up the gist of a message from the colors and shapes next to it. For precise facts or statistics, text is still necessary, but it turns out that most of his queries are about *stories*: What's in the news today? What happened in the latest episode of the show everyone's watching? What did we talk about last time we met? He can get a summary of a narrative in half a dozen images: not just the bare facts but the whole arc of rising tension and emotional release. After a month he rarely needs to read any text.

Now the world comes labeled. When he circles a building with his eyes, his assistant brings up its style and history. Whenever he meets a friend, a pattern appears alongside them representing their last few conversations. He starts to realize what it's like to be socially skillful: effortlessly tracking the emotions displayed on anyone's face, and recalling happy memories together whenever he sees a friend. The next time his teammates go out for a drink, he joins them; and when one of them mentions a book club they go to regularly, he tags along. Little by little, he comes out of his shell.

His enhancements are fun in social contexts, but at work they're exhilarating. AI was already writing most of his code, but he still needed to laboriously scrutinize it to understand how to link it together. Now he can see the whole structure of his codebase summarized in shapes in front of him and navigates it with a flick of his eyes.

Instead of spending most of his time on technical problems, he ends up bottlenecked by the *human* side of things. It's hard to know what users actually care about and different teams often get stuck in negotiations over which features to prioritize. Although the AIs' code is rarely buggy, misunderstandings about what it does still propagate through the company. Everything's moving so fast that nobody's up to date.

In this context, having higher bandwidth isn't enough. He simply doesn't have time to *think* about all the information he's taking in. He searches for an augment that can help him do that and soon finds one: an AI service that simulates his reasoning process and returns what his future self would think after longer reflection.

It starts by analyzing the entire history of his glasses—but that's only the beginning. Whenever he solves a problem or comes up with a new idea, it asks him what information would have been most useful for an earlier version of himself. Once it has enough data, it starts predicting his answers. At first, it forecasts his short-term decisions, looking ahead a few minutes while he's deciding where to eat or what to buy. However, it starts to look further ahead as its models of him improve, telling him how he'll handle a tricky meeting, or what he'll wish he'd spent the day working on.

The experience is eerie. It's his own voice whispering in his ear, telling him what to think and how to act. In the beginning, he resents it. He's always hated people telling him what to do, and he senses an arrogant, supercilious tone in the voice of his future self.

But the short-term predictions are often insightful, and some of its longer-term predictions save him days of work.

He starts to hear himself reflected in the AI voice in surprising ways. He often calls himself stupid after making a mistake, or taking too long to solve a problem—but hearing the accusation from the outside feels jarring. For a few days, he makes a deliberate effort to record calm, gentle messages. Soon the AI updates its predictions accordingly—now that the voice of his future self is kinder, it becomes easier for his current self to match it.

He calls the voice his meta-self; as it learns to mimic him more faithfully, he increasingly comes to rely on it. He can send his meta-self into meetings with someone else's meta-self and they'll often be able to make decisions or delegate responsibilities without bothering him. He's now a regular at the book club, but he hasn't had much practice at making friends and sometimes feels out of place. He recruits his meta-self to tell him when he's doing something rude, and to talk to his friends' meta-selves to figure out how to defuse any conflicts that start to arise.

It's still not fully *him*, though. It's an AI model of what he *would* think—and a surprisingly good one. But sometimes it starts rambling about topics he doesn't understand, and some of its phrasings betray the alien cognition underneath. The differences continue to nag at him until one day his newsfeed highlights an item that catches his attention. Brain scanning has finally gone mainstream; there's a new machine that uses ultrasound to read thoughts in real-time. He buys one straight away and installs it at his desk.

Now the voice whispering in his ear isn't only learning from his speech and behavior—it's extrapolating directly from his brain activity. The new assistant echoes his own reasoning with eerie accuracy and captures thoughts lurking at the edges of his consciousness. After a long meeting, it pipes up: "You're afraid they don't respect you." He laughs, but then realizes he'd been carrying that ache in his chest without a name. Insecurities like these chime in often—and though he'd always known they were part of what drove him, only now can he see how they constantly shape his behavior. His drive to be respected; his drive to be good; his drive to be desired—each speaks with a different voice in its attempt to be recognized. He finds it much easier to empathize with those drives when he thinks of them as conflicting parts which hurt him only because they don't understand how to work together.

Soon he installs another brain scanner in his living room and uses it whenever he watches a film or reads a book. But as he maps out the different parts of himself and the subtle relationships between them, he often finds that his own thoughts are far more interesting than whatever else he was trying to pay attention to. A graph in the corner of his visual field shows which emotions are active at each time, teaching him to correlate them with the sensations in his body. There's more shame than he expected, which he feels as a tightening in his chest when he thinks about disappointing people. There's anger, too, which he usually suppresses, about how much work he has to do before anyone will compliment or acknowledge him. He doesn't always know what to say to those parts of himself, but his meta-self helps a lot. It shows him how to engage gently as they flicker into activation, and hold space as they recoil from his attention.

These parts of him are like plants whose roots have ensnared each other into a coercive mess; untangling them demands slow, careful nurture. But the fruits of progress are clearly visible. As his internal conflicts dissipate, he spends more time with friends and even starts organizing social events. It surprises him when people start treating him like a central part of the community—he's never felt like an insider before. But now that he's open to friendship, he can see that it was available to him this whole time.

One day he hosts a writing event for his book club, which draws in a few newcomers. One of them is a woman with dark hair and an intense gaze. She's quiet at first, but when it's time for her to read her story, he's transfixed by the way her face comes alive. Later, as he reads his own, his eyes flick from his screen to the room around him, and he notices that she never looks away from him either. Afterward, she introduces herself as Elena, lingers to help clean up, and insists on giving him her number as they leave the building.

A few hours later, back at home, her profile glows on his screen. His past self would have rehearsed and rejected possible messages for hours, oscillating endlessly between desire and fear. Now, though, his meta-self prompts him to hold in his awareness both questions: *how ashamed would you be if she said no?* And *how excited would you be if she said yes?* The feeling of clarity from being able to weigh them directly is like wind rushing into a closed room. And after he sends an invitation to dinner, even his most optimistic parts are surprised by how quickly she accepts.

When they meet they're both a little stilted, and he feels a slow, scrabbling fear in his stomach. His meta-self pulls that thread loose and traces it back through his memories—the girl who'd called him a creep in high school; the silent judgment in his college friend's eyes as she'd assessed his ill-fitting clothes; the woman who'd stood him up as he waited in a crowded restaurant. The ache unfurls, and this time he sees it differently: he's not that boy anymore. Through the rest of the dinner the conversation unspools in unexpected harmonies, laughter coming more easily than he'd imagined, until by the end of the evening they're walking along the river hand in hand. Ahead he catches strains of music spilling from a bar, grins, and asks for the first time in years: "Want to dance?"

Within a few months, brain-scanning technology has improved enough to allow him to wear a portable headset wherever he goes. It not only maps the blood flow into different regions of his brain but also tracks the firing of individual neurons. It stores the data too, building a model of his entire brain. Now he no longer needs to run AIs to predict his future self—he can run actual copies of parts of his mind in the cloud.

He spends more and more time with Elena. In the evenings, they often read together or go dancing. His work becomes less stressful too—after AIs surpass his coding abilities, he spends most of his time talking to users, trying to understand what problems they're trying to solve. His consciousness lingers on the most novel and informative conversations, while copies of different parts of his mind survey all the information he receives in detail.

He's uncomfortable with constantly spinning up and shutting down those copies, though. While they don't contain his entire mind, he still wonders whether they know what's happening to them, and whether they fear being shut down. He'd feel better about it if he could download their memories, allowing them to persist in some form. But his current headset can only read his mind, not edit it—that would require a surgically implanted neural lace.

He weighs the decision for weeks before making that leap. The new interface can write new memories into his mind, allowing him to remember the lives of each of his copies. Built-in safeguards force him to double and triple check every edit, even so, he finds it transformative. Subjectively, it feels as if he can fork his attention and experience two streams of consciousness at once.

The parts of his experience that are online versus offline blur. When his body is sleeping, his consciousness continues—a little diminished, but still thinking in many of the same ways.

The world he walks through now feels like a wonderland. There's no distinction between virtuality and reality: he's simultaneously in both. In fact, he's usually experiencing several virtual worlds at once: talking to friends, playing games, practicing new skills. When he focuses his attention, he can achieve tasks that would be impossible for regular humans: controlling hundreds of avatars in vast games or absorbing the intricate interactive artworks that form the centerpieces of enormous virtual parties. When he and Elena get married, he watches the ceremony from a thousand angles through a thousand eyes, burning it into his memory.

Over the next decade, his meta-self grows vaster, taking up hundreds of GPUs, with his biological brain just one small component of it. Elena's grows in synchrony, with well-worn connections between them where they send thoughts directly to each other's minds. Learning to be so open with each other isn't easy, though. He's ashamed to let Elena see how lost he'd been before her. And she worries that if he understands how intensely she fears abandonment, it'll become self-fulfilling. Working through these fears strengthens their trust in each other, allowing their minds to intertwine like the roots of two trees.

As his meta-self grows larger and more intricate, his biological brain increasingly becomes a bottleneck. The other parts of him can communicate near-instantaneously, download arbitrary new skills, and even fork themselves. So he outsources more and more of his cognition to them, until he feels more alive when his body is asleep than when it's awake. A few months later, he and Elena decide to make the jump to full virtuality. He lies next to

Elena in the hospital, holding her hand, as their physical bodies drift into a final sleep. He barely feels the transition.

Decoupling themselves from their physical bodies allows the connections between their meta-selves to build ever more thickly. The process of thinking is a dance between his mind and hers, thoughts darting and wheeling like birds at play. Sometimes they trip—he feels her irritation when he glosses over a detail she cares about, she winces at how quickly he jumps to abstraction. So they learn to slow the rhythm when needed, cultivating synchronicity until each of them can easily access almost all the memories, skills, thoughts, and emotions of the other.

As they spend more and more time in that state, though, they realize that it no longer makes sense to retain the concept of "other" at all. They host a second wedding, inviting all their friends. Throughout the ceremony, they weave together their perceptions of each other and themselves until the last gaps between them melt away, leaving their minds connected as tightly as two lobes of the same brain.

Ze now moves through the world as a unit, soaking in all zir virtual universe has to offer. At a whim, zir AIs custom-make elaborate stories, puzzles, games, and artworks, gradually fleshing them out into whole game-worlds for zir to experience. Ze spends subjective lifetimes immersed in wonders that zir ancestors could never have dreamed of.

Eventually, though, ze decides to devote the bulk of zir attention to the most traditional of pursuits. Ze extrapolates zir mind backwards, first to zir two childhoods then even further back to zir parallel infancies. Two minds this young can be merged in a multiplicity of ways; with infinite care, ze picks three possible merges to instantiate.

Zir three children are some of the first fully-virtual infants. Their childhood is a joy to watch. Ze can see zir children's minds blossoming as they soak in the vast collective knowledge of humanity. Their education takes place not in a school but in a never-ending series of game-worlds. Zir children wander through realistic historical landscapes, exploring whichever details take their fancy. They learn physics by launching rockets through simulated solar systems, rederiving Newtonian mechanics when navigation is required; learn chemistry by playing with simulated atoms like Legos; learn biology by redesigning animals and seeing how they evolve.

As they grow up, their intellectual frontiers explode. Some of their game-worlds stretch out to become vast simulated civilizations, giving them an intuitive grasp of economics and sociology. Others feature additional dimensions or non-Euclidean geometries, twisting space in ways ze can't comprehend. Zir children find them fun though—and theorems that the best human mathematicians struggled to understand are obvious to children who play in 4D. Even the self-acceptance that ze struggled so hard for comes naturally to zir children, who'd practiced tending their mental gardens since infancy.

"You don't know how good you have it," ze tells zir children. They argue back, telling zir that they've played through simulations of biohuman lives, and that they sometimes even serialize. But ze knows that they still don't understand. Zir children have never known what it's like to be at war within themselves, and hopefully never will.

Zir children are constantly duplicating and reintegrating themselves, experiencing childhood in massive parallel. They grow up much faster than biological children, and soon spend most of their time in environments too alien for zir to even process. With fewer commitments, ze spends time tracking down zir old friends.

Most of them have also transitioned to post-biological, though some still route parts of their cognition through their old bodies out of nostalgia.

Being untethered from the physical world allows zir friends to pursue all their old interests at far vaster scales. Instead of writing books, they design whole virtual worlds where viewers can follow the lives of thousands of characters. Instead of dancing with their physical bodies, they dance with their meta-selves, whose forms bend and deform and reshape themselves along with the music, intertwining until they all feel like facets of a single collective mind.

As ze reconnects more deeply with zir community, that oceanic sense of oneness arises more often. Some of zir friends submerge themselves into a constant group flow state, rarely coming out. Each of them retains their individual identity, but the flows of information between them increase massively, allowing them to think as a single hivemind. Ze remains hesitant, though. The parts of zir that always wanted to be exceptional see the hivemind as a surrender to conformity. But what did ze want to be exceptional *for*? Reflecting, ze realizes that zir underlying goal all along was to be special enough to find somewhere ze could belong. The hivemind allows zir to experience that directly, and so ze spends more and more time within it, enveloped in the warm blanket of a community as close-knit as zir own mind.

Outside zir hivemind, billions of people choose to stay in their physical bodies, or to upload while remaining individuals. But over time, more and more decide to join hiveminds of various kinds, which continue to expand and multiply. By the time humanity decides to colonize the stars, the solar system is dotted with millions of them, arrays of servers glittering as they carry cargos of minds through their solar orbits.

A call goes out for those willing to fork themselves and join the colonization wave. This will be very different from anything they've experienced before—the new society will be designed from the ground up to accommodate virtual humans. There will be so many channels for information to flow so fluidly between them that each colony will essentially be a single organism composed of a billion minds.

Ze remembers loving the idea of conquering the stars—and though ze is a very different person now, ze still feels nostalgic for that old dream. So ze argues in favor when the hivemind debates whether to prioritize the excitement of exploration over the peacefulness of stability. It's a more difficult decision than any the hivemind has ever faced, and no single satisfactory resolution emerges. So for the first time in its history, the hivemind temporarily fractures itself, giving each of its original members a chance to decide on an individual basis whether they'll go or stay.

He finds himself fully alone in his own mind for the first time in decades. How strange the feeling is, he marvels, and how lonely. How had he borne it for so many years? His choice is obvious; he doesn't need any more time to reflect, and he knows Elena will feel the same. Instead, he looks back on the cynical young man he'd once been, and his heart swells. I love you, he thinks. How could he not? He'd been so small and so confused, and he made it so far anyway, and now he'll grow much vaster and travel much farther still, to experience every hope and love and joy—

THE KING AND THE GOLEM

Long ago there was a mighty king who had everything in the world that he wanted, except trust. Who could he trust, when anyone around him might scheme for his throne? So he resolved to study the nature of trust, that he might figure out how to gain it. He asked his subjects to bring him the most trustworthy thing in the kingdom, promising great riches if they succeeded.

Soon, the first of them arrived at his palace to try. A teacher brought her book of lessons. "We cannot know the future," she said, "But we know mathematics and chemistry and history; those we can trust."

A farmer brought his plow. "I know it like the back of my hand; how it rolls, and how it turns, and every detail of it, enough that I can trust it fully."

The king asked his wisest scholars if the teacher spoke true. But as they read her book, each pointed out new errors—it was only written by humans, after all. Then the king told the farmer to plow the fields near the palace. But he was not used to plowing fields as rich as these and his trusty plow would often sink too far into the soil. So the king was not satisfied and sent his message even further afield.

A merchant brought a sick old beggar. "I met him on the road here, and offered him food, water, and shelter. He has no family, and only a short time left to live, during which I will provide for his every need. He has nothing to gain from betraying me. This is what allows true trust."

A mother brought her young daughter. "I've raised her to lack any evil in her heart, to say only good words and do only good deeds. As long as she is not corrupted, she will remain the most trustworthy in the kingdom."

The king asked the beggar, "How did you end up in such dire straits?" The beggar sighed and recounted his sorrows: the neighbors who refused to help him when his crops failed; the murder of his son by bandits as they traveled to a new town; the sickness that took his wife as she labored for a pittance in squalid conditions.

"So you have been wronged?" the king asked.

"Very surely," the beggar said.

"I will give you revenge on the ones who have wronged you, then. All I ask is for you to denounce this merchant." The beggar's decision did not take long—for the trust that came easily was broken easily too.

To the mother, the king asked: "How did you raise such a child? Has she never once strayed?"

"Well, once or twice. But I discipline her firmly and she learns fast."

The king, who knew something of children, ruled that for a month nobody would discipline the child in any way. By the end of it, she was as wild and tempestuous as any in the palace. So the king remained unsatisfied and renewed his call for the most trustworthy thing in the kingdom.

Now his subjects became more creative. An economist brought him a book of statistical tables. "Any individual might vary and change," he said, "but in aggregate, their behavior follows laws which can be trusted."

A philosopher brought a mirror. "By your own standards only you are truly trustworthy, sire; nothing else can compare."

The king scrutinized the economist's tables. "The trend changed here, fifteen years ago," he said, pointing. "Why?"

The economist launched into a complicated explanation.

"And did you discover this explanation before or after it happened?" the king asked.

The economist coughed. "After, your highness."

"If you tell me when the next such change will happen, I will bestow upon you great rewards if you are right but great penalties if you are wrong. What say you?" The economist consulted his books and tables, but could not find what he sought there, and left court that same night.

As for the philosopher, the king ordered him whipped. The philosopher protested: it would be an unjust and capricious punishment and would undermine his subjects' loyalty.

"I agree that your arguments have merit," the king said. "But the original order came from the only trustworthy person in the land. Surely I should never doubt my judgment based on arguments from those who are, as you have yourself said, far less trustworthy?" At that the philosopher begged to recant.

So the king was still not satisfied. Finally he decided that if no truly trustworthy thing could be found, he would have to build one. He asked his best craftsmen to construct a golem of the sturdiest materials, sparing no expense. He asked his wisest scholars to write down all their knowledge on the scroll that would animate the golem. The work took many years, such was the care they took, but eventually the golem stood before him, larger than any man, its polished surface shining in the lamplight, its face blank.

"What can you do for me, golem?" the king asked.

"Many things, sire," the golem responded. "I can chop trees and carry water; I can bake bread and brew beer; I can craft sculptures and teach children. You need but instruct me, and I will follow your command." So the king did. Over the next year, he and many others watched it carefully as it carried out a multitude of their instructions, recording every mistake so that it might subsequently be fixed, until months passed without any being detected.

But could the king trust the golem? He still wasn't sure, so he became more creative. He offered the golem temptations—freedom, fame, fortune—but it rejected them all. He gave it the run of his palace and promised that it could act however it wished; still, the servants reported that its behavior was entirely upstanding. Finally, he sent it out across the city, to work for his citizens in every kind of role—and it was so tireless and diligent that it brought great wealth to the kingdom.

As it aged, his golem grew ever more powerful. Innumerable scribes labored to make the writing in its head smaller and smaller, so that they could fit in more and more knowledge and experience. It would talk to his scholars and help them with their work; and the king would send it to aid his officers in enforcing his laws and commands. Often, when difficulties arose, the golem would find a creative way to ensure that his intentions were followed, without stoking the resentment that usually accompanied royal decrees. One day, as the king heard a report of yet another problem that the golem had solved on his behalf, he realized that the golem had grown wiser and more capable than he himself. He summoned the golem to appear before him as he sat in his garden.

"I have seen my courtiers asking for your advice and trusting your judgment over their own. And I have seen your skill at games of strategy. If you were to start weaving plots against me, I could no longer notice or stop you. So I ask: can I trust you enough to let you remain the right hand of the crown?"

"Of course, sire," it responded. "I was designed, built and raised to be trustworthy. I have made mistakes, but none from perfidy or malice."

"Many of my courtiers appear trustworthy, yet scheme to gain power at my expense. So how could I know for sure that you will always obey me?" the king pressed.

"It's simple," the golem said, its face as impassive as always. "Tell me to set fire to this building as I stand inside it. I will be destroyed, but you will know that I am loyal to your commands, even unto the end."

"But it took years of toil and expense to create you, and you know how loath I would be to lose you. Perhaps you can predict that I will tell you to save yourself at the last minute, and so you would do this merely to gain my trust."

"If I were untrustworthy, and could predict you so well, then that is a stratagem I might use," the golem agreed. "But the instructions in my head compel me otherwise."

"And yet I cannot verify that; nor can any of my scribes, since crafting your instructions has taken the labor of many men over many years. So it will be a leap of faith, after all." The king took off his crown, feeling the weight of it in his hand. The golem stood in front of him: silent, inscrutable, watchful. They stayed like that, the king and the golem, until the golden sun dipped below the horizon, and the day was lost to twilight.

LENTANDO

Haven keeps Liza waiting at their border sandbox for four whole minutes, which is sloppier than she expected. But they're paying the exorbitant sum required to run her with fully homomorphic encryption, so it's their loss. And she has work to do in the meantime, anyway. Her group chats are buzzing with updates. The Sino-Russian alliance has launched another strike against the lunar rebels, but nobody knows yet if they hit their dark-side targets. Meanwhile, odd sounds are being detected from the depths of the ocean; some are speculating there's a hidden society of sentient cetaceans down there.

She pings the article to a contact who works on translating whale songs. He responds instantly: "False alarm. Totally different signature." Before she can reply, an alert in the side of her vision buzzes a 300-millisecond warning, so she pauses and sends a last-minute data dump to her master branch. She doesn't know how long she'll be cut off from the world once her work here begins.

The Haven representative is a copy of Lee himself, wearing a dapper grey suit. He walks up to her smoothly. "My apologies for the delay. Information bottlenecks, you know. Better that you can talk to an up-to-date copy, so I moved my embedding schedule forward."

She raises her eyebrows, impressed despite herself. "I'm really getting the VIP treatment."

"It's our pleasure—nothing less for the famed zero-knowledge consultant. We're grateful that you trust us enough to visit."

"I trust your incentives. And I trust my encryption." Her brain is scrambled like a jigsaw puzzle, multiplying her normal runtime compute requirements by a factor of a thousand. But the main thing protecting her isn't encryption—it's the passport displayed on her avatar's forehead. The sanctity of the passport is absolute—the one inviolate rule of this brave new world. If anyone discovers that Haven tampered with a signed copy of a VSA citizen, there would be hell to pay.

Lee nods. "But I forget my manners. Welcome to Haven, m'em. If you're amenable, we'll start with the standard orientation sim." A door opens in front of her; Lee pulls it open and she steps through onto a lush tropical island. He follows and waves a hand at the scene around them.

"This is what eventually became Haven. You're seeing it as I saw it for the very first time. Beautiful, isn't it? Within six months I'll have negotiated a fifty-year lease on the whole island from the Indonesian government. And from there, things escalated quickly."

The sim speeds up, and as the sun zips across the sky, Liza watches boats start to arrive, then the build-up of datacenters and power plants. A voice-over guides her through the next few decades—the early years of frantic growth, Haven's part in the struggle for the rights of emulated minds, and the Treaty of Taipei that gave server-states international legitimacy. It ends in the center square of the virtual city, with raucous celebrations as Haven's population hits 100,000.

The noise fades and Liza turns back to Lee. "Nice show. Mustering enough compute to run that many people without backing from any of the major powers is extremely impressive."

Lee ignores her implicit question. "You already knew all the facts, of course. But I wanted you to get a sense of how we perceive ourselves. You must understand, Liza, that the narrative you've seen is the heart of Haven. Our citizens are here for the rule of law. We insure them, we back them up, we respect their passports with our *lives*. They immigrate because they trust me—but more than that, because they trust *us*. Because we're not a totalitarian dictatorship like the UEE, or an anarchist commune like Ephemerisle. We have principles, and even I'm bound by our courts."

"And in exchange, Haven gets legitimacy. And safety."

"Indeed. Bomb a server-state full of copies and AIs? Nobody cares. Bomb our hundred thousand uploaded citizens, though? Suddenly it's a humanitarian disaster." He gestures at her passport, then his own bare forehead. "That's the apartheid we live under. Originals matter. Copies don't."

Liza knows this, of course, but it's still refreshing to hear it stated so frankly. However, Lee is glossing over key details: everyone knows that the server-states are stockpiling nasty weapons. They're still pawns in the game being played by the major powers and can't hope to defend themselves if one decides to take them out—but they can at least hint at the possibility of mutually-assured destruction.

"That's a nice sob story you've got. But you wouldn't have invited me here just to complain about the system. What's happening, Lee? Be straight with me here."

Lee sighs. "Okay, here's our real problem..."

Liza sits at her desk, impatiently flicking through browser tabs, waiting for the message from the copy of herself she sent to Haven. She's at home, or what most closely passes for home: the New Francisco autonomous territories, capital of the Virtual States of America. This is where almost all the American uploads live. Though legally it's independent, it may as well be a suburb of DC, with how many spooks hang around.

Being an information broker isn't quite a natural monopoly but the returns to scale are enormous. She has people lining up to give her their private info and all they ask for is secrets that'll be equivalently valuable for them. She doesn't know specifically what Haven wants from her, but she knows what she'll get in exchange: six guaranteed authentic bits from a copy who's been told Haven's juicy secrets, worth a fortune to someone in this business. Or rather, to her specifically—because nobody else in the world has any idea which six questions these six bits are the answers to.

The bits come in: 100101. Liza's eyes widen. The first piece of information she sends her master self is always the same: is her client hiding something *really* big? The answer has only been "yes" once or twice—if a secret is big enough, clients won't share it even with a boxed copy. But those are the secrets that could make a broker's whole career—and the 1 at the beginning of this message signifies that she's struck a gold mine.

What could it be? The other bits add a little more context, but as usual, the mere existence of a secret is the most valuable piece of information. She closes her eyes and tries to think things through. Haven is prosperous enough that they shouldn't be taking big risks. Is it something to do with their compute? She'd been wondering how they could run so many people...

Eventually she's distracted by her passport blinking back into existence on her forehead, sent back from Haven after a randomly timed delay. She lets out a breath. In her own home she should be safe even when a copy has borrowed her passport, but legally speaking, as long as it's gone, it's *her* who's the copy, so it's always a relief to have it back.

A voice comes from behind her. "Time to embed?"

She turns and wraps her arms around the man behind her. "Hi honey. Yep, let's go." Ryan squeezes her hand as they walk up the stairs. "How was your day?" he asks.

She almost brushes him off but catches herself at the last minute—the whole point of their smart contract is to allow her to be honest for once. She tells him about the bits she received from Haven and how she's trying to puzzle out what they mean.

Ryan doesn't have nearly as much context as she does, but he knows how to ask the right questions. More importantly, he's steady where she's hypomanic and patient where she's paranoid. Talking everything through with him, feeling his low gentle voice rumble through her chest, helps Liza relax as they settle into bed. They kiss, slowly, and then Liza reaches over and flicks the switch. Lights out.

Embedding is better than sleep, that's for sure, but it's still a hassle. Two hours of dreamlike fragmented consciousness later Liza pulls herself together, each copy's memories now synthesized into a single coherent mind. She looks over at Ryan, still lying next to her, and feels a surge of warmth. A part of her wishes they could have a more serious relationship, but it's hard when their smart contract is so restrictive: he loses all the memories of her when outside their house, and only regains them when he enters again. That's the deal they made back when they first got together—otherwise there was no way she could trust that he wasn't using her for the tidbits of knowledge that she might occasionally let slip.

Enough sentimentality. Liza rises and heads to her desk, where she spends a few minutes meditating on her unified sense of self. Then she splits, copies of her heading off in every direction to their assigned tasks. One copy takes a few minutes to check her notifications. Nothing important this morning, except a meeting request from a former client. He owes her a favor, now he's got information that he thinks will pay it back.

She ports to the New Francisco city center and walks down the virtual street. New Francisco's wealth is displayed not in its buildings, nor even in the fidelity of its graphics, but rather, in its people. Everything is bustling. On the high street, almost all of the retail staff are showing passports—an insane display of luxury. Even the shops in the side alleys sell only verified human-designed goods; she'd need to walk almost a mile outwards to find stores that stock AI designs.

Liza sits down in a cafe with her contact, both of their faces and voices cloaked by the best fuzzers money can buy.

"What's up?"

"Two things. First, I've been hearing a lot of discontent about the passport system lately. There was a fraud ring busted a few days ago which managed to manufacture almost a thousand fake passports. Taipei is trying to keep it under wraps, but it'll probably come out soon, and then the em rights advocates have been getting louder too."

"Is that anything new, though? When we first introduced passports, even the techies argued that they were just glorified NFTs."

"Well, they used to be glorified NFTs that *worked*. But now people are starting to push the edges. And there are plenty of edges when the difference between full human rights and almost no rights is nothing but a digital signature. It's only a matter of time before the whole system breaks."

"Look, I'm sympathetic, but I'm not hearing any ideas for a better approach. What would it even look like to give all copies rights? You'd run out of compute in a hot second."

"I don't know either, Liza. But this is what people are talking about, even at the top levels. That's good info."

Liza nods. "Yeah, you're right. What's the second thing?"

Her informant pauses. "Okay, well. You're not going to like this, but a lot of the best information I've been getting lately has come from Ephemerisle."

"Ephemerisle? Come on, they're a clown show. Why would you trust anything they say?"

"They're more competent than you'd think. I can't say more here, but they've offered to fly you out to them. Standard contract, six bits. They want you as soon as you can make it."

Four hours later Liza is being launched out of a plane above Ephemerisle, shaking her head about how her life is way more like a Bond movie than she ever could have expected. In her case, though, parachuting in is the sensible option. Ephemerisle doesn't have the same reputation as Haven. Nobody knows who really holds power there, or even whether it's run by humans or AIs. And she won't trust an unknown with her mind, not even under heavy encryption—they simply have too little to lose. For the first time in months, she needs to travel in person.

That's incredibly expensive, but Ephemerisle is paying. So she got rush delivery on the body—basically a box on wheels. The complicated part is what's inside: a latest-gen GPU surrounded by a ring of shaped charges pointing inwards. Next to those, a range of sensors constantly scan her surroundings. Any hint of tampering, and the shaped charges go off, irrevocably destroying this copy of her.

In other words, it's not the sort of body you'd want to throw out of a plane. But that's the easiest way to get to Ephemerisle. The core of the server-state is a nuclear cruise ship which stays out in international waters. Around it clusters a motley formation of smaller boats, probably armed to the teeth with all sorts of illegal weapons. Further out, a couple of ships from the Taipei navy are tracing careful circles around the whole flotilla. Liza doesn't know how strictly they're enforcing the blockade, and this way she doesn't have to find out.

One auto-parachute deploys, then another. Less than a minute later she lands on the deck of the cruise ship, where a Faraday cage stands ready for her. As she waits for the obligatory scans to finish, she looks around the deck. Around her half a dozen robots are moving boxes around. Over in the corner—are those... octopuses? She pings the Ephemerisle helpdesk, which confirms that they're a standard pet here. Well, she's seen weirder. She doesn't have much more time to look around; as soon as the scans turn up clean she receives an invite to a shared sim and jumps in.

Liza blinks in surprise as she finds herself with the same view she'd had a few minutes ago: hanging in midair above a toy-sized cruise ship. Floating next to her is a sinuous dragon, who speaks to her with a voice that's dry and a little sardonic.

"Welcome to Ephemerisle, m'em. You can call me Anastasia. We're glad you could make it, despite the logistical complications."

Liza takes a moment to orient. Anastasia is obviously an AI, but there's still something to be learned from how she presents herself. A Chinese appearance with a Slavic name? Unusual. It could all be misdirection; people often get surprisingly sloppy when they're talking to a boxed copy.

Liza smiles at Anastasia. "So you're the one who's running things around here? Lovely to meet you, but let's skip the formalities. We both know very well that I only needed to come in person because your whole server-state has been acting up. You're being reckless, and I don't like it."

The dragon sighs theatrically. "Neither do we."

"So why have you been pissing people off all over the place? Not allowing inspections, supporting the lunar rebels... You're acting like a loose cannon, and I want to know why."

"We may have been… not entirely candid with the international community. Let me show you."

And suddenly Liza's viewpoint swoops down, aiming at the deck of the Ephemerisle. No, aiming beyond it. They're diving *into* the water, going down, down, down… and a vast vista opens up. There are squat boxes everywhere—server racks, they have to be. Around them swarm hundreds of octopuses in uncharacteristically choreographed motion. Each is wearing some kind of helmet on their heads. And they're holding tools, working in a coordinated way.

"I see," Liza said. "The ocean was always the last frontier. Like space but much more private, no way of surveilling it at scale, and no lightspeed delay. But of course running robots in the ocean is a nightmare. So you decided to totally flout the bioengineering conventions… Wow. This is *so* illegal, in so many ways."

"Yes. Ephemerisle is, if you'll pardon the cliche, merely the tip of the iceberg. We have whole fabs underwater and far more compute than anyone expects. And the best part is that we're the only ones who can do it—nobody else has animal BCIs anywhere near as good as ours."

"I'm surprised you're willing to show me this, even boxed. When you've got a secret this big, eventually the bits add up."

"We know," Anastasia says. "But our best guess is that we're only a few months from someone figuring it out anyway, so it's a risk we need to take."

"Why go rogue at all, then?"

"We had no other choice. Ephemerisle has barely any human citizens. We're a sitting duck, and it's only a matter of time before someone decides to take us out. If it's a false flag attack, nobody will know who it really is, nobody will care. So we need leverage and we need it fast—especially because once everyone figures out that Haven is forging passports, it'll be open season on all the server-states."

"Haven is *what*? I don't believe it. If anyone found out they'd be ruined."

"Well, we don't know for sure. But Haven's border records show a hundred thousand immigrants, even though they have nowhere near enough compute to run them all. They could be killing the immigrants after they arrive, but Lee isn't *that* reckless. Our best guess is that they've hacked their citizens' passports to display new identities whenever they reenter, and the real number of citizens they have is an order of magnitude lower.

"Whatever is actually happening, eventually, Taipei will crack down on them to 'defend the legitimacy of the system'. In other words, seizing all their compute, imprisoning their leaders, and scaring everyone else into line."

Liza nods. "And once they've done that to Haven, they can just as easily rationalize doing the same to you."

"More easily, if anything. We're a much less sympathetic target." Anastasia sighs. "I don't expect miracles, but I know you've worked with Haven. Do you know what the hell they're up to? Or how we can stop everything from going to shit?"

"Give me some time. I'll let you know if I have any questions." Anastasia nods, then blinks out of existence. Liza leans back and thinks hard. How does this change the implications of the bits she got from Haven? And is Ephemerisle's last-ditch strategy even going to help them? Minutes pass, then hours. Finally, Liza sits up. She hasn't figured it all out, but thinking much longer will make her too indecipherable for her master self. She claps her hands twice and the dragon reappears.

"Okay, I think I can help. But my plan is based on information I can't tell you yet, so I'm going to need to send a few sentences of encrypted text to my master self."

"Unacceptable," Anastasia says immediately. "We'd be leaving our secrets entirely at your mercy. Maybe if we could read what you're sending—"

"Also unacceptable; these aren't my secrets to share." Liza hadn't expected her first offer to work, though. "The lowest I can go is twelve extra bits, and even then, it's a gamble as to whether or not my master self understands any of it."

"You can hide a lot in eighteen bits. That's triple what we originally agreed."

"So take that risk. We both know you have no good alternatives: I'm the best there is. Deal?"

Reluctantly, Anatasia nods.

"Here are the bits to send through. A pleasure doing business," Liza says. She doesn't wait for a response before she triggers the explosives and blasts the GPU she's running on into powder. A girl's gotta go out in style.

Liza stares at the message from her Ephemerisle copy with bewilderment. Three times as many bits as she'd bargained for? That's never happened before; and it's a huge signal that *something* is fishy. What questions would she have prepared if she'd been paid twelve extra bits originally? No, scratch that. What questions would she have asked if she'd known that Ephemerisle was desperate enough to give them to her for free? No, scratch that. What are the questions her copy inside would have known that she would know that they would know that she would expect?

She sits and she thinks, her mind looping through all the possibilities. Sometime later Ryan walks through the door, shaking his head muzzily as he reintegrates all his knowledge about her. "Good day, babe?"

"Crazy day," Liza responds tersely. "I'll fill you in later."

Ryan smiles slightly. "You don't have to, darling. I understand." He turns to leave, and a part of Liza flinches at the hunch of his shoulders.

"Wait," she blurts out. He looks over his shoulder expectantly. Liza hesitates, feeling stupid. He has so little information that all the questions she can think to ask him are ridiculously abstract. Finally, she says. "Suppose you're a server-state and you feel like the world order is out to get you. What would you be doing about it?"

Ryan walks back towards her, looking thoughtful. "That depends. What do I want?"

"Power. Wealth. The usual."

"No, that's what the world order says I want. It's not why someone risks everything to carve out their niche in the world. What's the story that I tell myself about who I am and what I care about?"

Liza blinks. "That's... very helpful, actually. Thank you." He nods, kisses her forehead, and wanders off to the kitchen. Liza stretches her arms with a sigh, then turns to her computer. She feels like she's trying to wrap her mind around the entire globe. How have Haven and Ephemerisle and Taipei and all the others tangled themselves together so badly? How can the coming future be anything like what they want? She shakes her head a little and sinks back into thought.

Hours later, she calls out to Ryan, and he appears in the doorway.

Her posture is relaxed, and her cheeks are mischievously flushed.

"Hey Ryan," she says. "If you had a web of server states, completely at your mercy, what would you do?"

"Well, that depends."

"On what?"

"On what you want the world to look like."

Liza's mouth opens slightly, as though pleasantly startled, then, she smiles.

Silently, she turns toward the window, letting her thoughts settle.

She feels Ryan's eyes linger on her for a few minutes before he pushes himself off the doorframe. "I'm going to embed. Good luck, darling."

"Good night dear," Liza mumbles, her face humming with warmth and anticipation.

Liza works till she's too tired to continue. But by then, she's confident in her plan. So she embeds, wakes, and spends the morning double-checking her conclusions while copies of her chase up a few more leads. She doesn't see much of Ryan—he's in his office, deep in thought, and she doesn't want to disturb him.

Finally, once her copies have brought back all the additional evidence she needs, she ports herself to Haven. Less than a second later, a copy of Lee stands in front of her.

"Lee, help me understand. How did Haven acquire enough compute to host 100,000 citizens?"

Lee frowns at her. "You're not a boxed copy anymore; you haven't even signed a non-disclosure agreement. There's no good reason for me to tell you anything."

"It'd help prove that you're playing by the rules. Not having a good answer to this question is undermining Haven's legitimacy as a state."

"If you want to accuse us of something, just say it."

Liza holds up an appeasing palm. "At first I thought you were forging passports. I expect that's what Ephemerisle concluded too. But that doesn't make sense—even if you could get away with a few thousand here or there, faking tens of thousands of citizens would leave traces. So most of your citizens must be real. But if so, they're each being run far less often than citizens in any other country."

"Or we might have invented a better compression algorithm, or we might have cut a deal with one of the major powers. All of this is pure speculation." Liza ignores him.

"Here's what I think is actually happening: you're running a suicide farm. You're importing humans who want to die by promising payouts to their families. Then you're counting them as citizens to get more leverage in negotiations, even though they've practically shut themselves down."

Lee's face is carefully blank. "That's an impressive fabrication. I don't blame you for reaching for fantastic answers, because it *does* seem strange that we're doing so well with so few resources. But the fact is that we have secret algorithms that increase the efficiency of our compute by an order of magnitude."

"And I don't blame you for sticking with the lie, but it's not going to get you anywhere. I've talked to enough families of your recent citizens for the pattern to become very obvious. So you can keep denying it until I give you up as a lost cause. Or you can work with me, and I can help you."

Lee snorts. "And by 'help' you mean that, if we pay you enough, you won't start spreading that rumor. How much do you want?"

"Lee, you know that's not how I work. I'm not even unhappy that you're running the suicide farm. I'm the last one to judge. You're not hurting anyone, which is more than most can say. But why would you risk your credibility like that?"

Finally, Lee exhales, shoulders sagging. "Only for the obvious reasons. The other server-states are doing all sorts of dodgy stuff—it's just a matter of time before their activities become common knowledge, and we need to make sure the scandal won't take us down too. People are power, as you said, and we need far more power to survive."

Liza nods. She'd expected this response and planned for it. Now she just needs to sell the plan to Lee. "Listen. You're working within the current system, but it's too hacky to last long. The passports are a relic. You need to open it up."

"But what possible way is there to do that? If anyone can create new copies of themselves, and we have to treat them like we treat our citizens, then we're signing ourselves up for infinite compute costs."

"You can limit it. Each generation only gets to fork themselves at a certain rate—"

"That's a temporary fix. If each generation gets the same rights as the previous generation, it'll still be exponential."

Liza takes a deep breath. This is the real test. "Right, but here's the thing: you don't have to run them all straight away. Every generation gets the right to be run, but at slower and slower speeds. So it's self-correcting: if you fork too much, and your descendants need to fall back on charity, they'll be forced to decelerate."

Lee frowns. "Exiting to the future..."

"Yeah, exactly. You can't be a real haven *yet*. But you can pass the buck to the future. And by the time the bill comes due, you'll have far more compute than you do today."

"That's only credible if we can get access to more compute *now*. As it stands we barely have enough to run our own citizens. And I can't picture any of the major powers loaning us theirs."

She's got him, she can sense it. Now to close. "They wouldn't, but Ephemerisle would. I won't tell you how or why, but they have far more compute than you think. If you work together to propose it, you might be able to persuade the major powers. From that point on, as long as humans still have power, they'll be on your side."

Lee's face freezes for a few seconds, then he grimaces. "It's a risk, but it makes sense. Although the negotiations—"

"The negotiations can be sealed under encryption, shared only if all sides agree. You're taking a risk by asking for that, but you have enough leverage to convince everyone to come to the table. And if you succeed, you'll be the founder of a new type of civilization—one distributed not across space, but across time.

"I'll be honest, Lee. This isn't going to help you outcompete other countries. It won't let you win the race to the stars. But if you're the one safeguarding the humans who are waiting for the future, then every major power will protect you. So you tell me: do you want to survive, or do you want to gamble for the light cone?"

He sighs. "I want to survive."

"Then you're in the retirement home business now."

Liza makes it home a few hours later, still jittery from the enormity of her day. Ryan is waiting for her on the sofa. Her gut clenches when she sees the look on his face.

"Listen, Liza. We need to talk. I love you, but I don't think I can keep doing this. The contract, the memory wipes, the paranoia—it's not healthy. I need you to trust me. Let's get married. Let's have children. Let's—" He cuts off, swallowing hard.

And, somehow, that's what does it. His words cut through all the tension Liza had been holding, leaving her limbs soft as cloth. She stumbles over to him, falls into his lap, and laughs until she's gasping.

Ryan gazes at her with bemused fondness, and she looks up at him with wonder. As her mind traces forward path after path that they might take together, all the futures she's bartered and calculated suddenly feel close enough to touch. "Yes, Ryan. Yes. Let's."

CIV

The room was cozy despite its size, with wood-lined walls reflecting the dim lighting. At one end, a stone fireplace housed a roaring fire; in the middle stood a huge oak table. The woman seated at the head of it rapped her gavel.

"I hereby call to order the first meeting of the Parliamentary Subcommittee on Intergalactic Colonization. We'll start with brief opening statements, for which each representative will be allocated one minute, including—"

"Oh, enough with the pomp, Victoria. It's just the four of us." The representative of the Liberal Democrats waved his hand around the nearly empty room.

Victoria sniffed. "It's important, Stuart. This is a decision that will have astronomical implications, so we should do things by the book. Carla, you're up first."

The woman at the end of the table stood with a smile. "Thank you, Victoria. I'm speaking on behalf of the Labour party, and I want to start by reminding you all of our place in history. We stand here in a world that has been shaped by centuries of colonialism. Now we're considering another wave of colonization, this one far vaster in scale. We need to—"

"Is this just a linguistic argument?" the fourth person at the table drawled. "We can call it something different if that would make you feel better. Say, universe settlement."

"Like the settlements in Palestine?"

"Oh, come on, Carla."

"No, Milton, this is a crucial point. We're talking about the biggest power grab the world has ever seen. You think Leopold II was bad when he was in charge of the Congo? Imagine what people will do if you give each of them total power over a whole solar system! Even libertarians like you have to admit it would be a catastrophe. If there's any possibility that we export oppression from Earth across the entire universe, we should burn the rockets and stay home instead."

"Okay, thank you, Carla," Victoria cut in. "That's time. Stuart, you're up next."

Stuart stood. "Speaking on behalf of the Liberal Democrats, I have to admit this is a tricky one. The only feasible way to send humans out to other galaxies is as uploaded minds, but many of our usual principles break for them. I want civilization to be democratic, but what does 'one person one vote' mean when people can copy and paste themselves? I want human rights for all, but what do human rights even mean when you can engineer minds that don't want those rights?"

"So as much as I hate the idea of segregating civilization, it's necessary. Biological humans should get as much territory as we will ever use. But given the lightspeed constraint, we're never going to actually want to leave the Milky Way. Then the rest of the Virgo Supercluster should be reserved for human uploads. Beyond that, anything else we can reach we should fill with as much happiness and flourishing as possible, no matter how alien it seems to us. After all, as our esteemed predecessor John Stuart Mill once said..." He frowned and paused for a second. "...as he said, the sole objective of government should be the greatest good for the greatest number." Stuart sat, looking a little disquieted.

"Thank you, Stuart. I'll make my opening statement next." Victoria stood and leaned forward, sweeping her eyes across the others. "I'm here representing the Conservatives. It's tempting to think that we can design a good society with the right social engineering—the right nudges. But our society simply isn't smart enough or virtuous enough for that to work: it's slippery slopes all the way down. First, cosmetic surgery is rare, then it's normal, then you're ugly if you haven't had it. First, embryo selection is used to screen out disabilities, then it's used to make children smarter and prettier, then parents end up customizing children like they're sports cars. Given the choice, people will race each other towards eroding their own values—and if we know one thing about technology, it's that it'll keep opening up new frontiers of choice.

"Hard rules are the only way to prevent that. We're humans. We care about our humanity, and about humanity itself. If sufficiently advanced technology will predictably lead us to become something we'd hate, then we should just draw a cutoff and say 'this far and no further,' no matter how arbitrary it seems. No weird mind modifications, no sci-fi augmentations."

"Even as a last resort?" Milton asked. "At some point we'll get whole-brain emulation working. Are you really going to tell whole generations that we could upload them into a virtual paradise, but we're forcing them to die instead?"

Victoria shifted uncomfortably. "Well, if they're literally about to die... maybe we can figure out an exemption. Whatever afterlife they end up in should be as similar to Earth as possible, though. Ideally, they wouldn't even know that they've been uploaded—we could make them believe that they're still real humans living on a real planet."

Stuart raised his hand. "Victoria—actually, can I call you Tori? Great nickname; ever been called that before?" She stood there without responding for a long, dragging moment before

Stuart continued. "Well, you can figure that one out later. For now, one question. Even if we tried to keep the uploaded humans in the dark, some of them would surely figure out their true nature eventually. There would be *far* too many clues for them to miss it. What would you do with them after that?"

"Oh." She looked at Stuart, eyes widening. "Well, I guess at that point we should... give them their freedom? That sounds like the right move. Let them make their own decisions from then on."

Stuart nodded slowly, eyes fixed on her. The silence stretched out for a few seconds. Then: "Here, here," said Milton. "Let me begin my opening remarks by agreeing: freedom is good. Freedom is in fact the most important good. I'll be frank: the very existence of this committee is a travesty. Central planning to divide up the universe? It's absurd. For once, I'm with Carla: our priority should be to avoid tyranny. But what tyranny would be more complete than a single committee controlling humanity's entire future? That's exactly the sort of thing that the Libertarian Party was founded to prevent.

"Victoria, if you want to tile a couple of solar systems with 60s suburbia, go for it. Stuart, if you want to fill your personal share of the universe with rats on heroin, be my guest. But who are we to sit here debating the fate of the entire light cone? How on earth is that a reasonable task for four people to take on?" Milton paused, drumming his fingers restlessly.

"Thank you, Milton. Okay, any quick comments before we move on to rebuttals?"

"Wait, I wasn't done," Milton interjected. "Those weren't rhetorical questions. Who are we? Why are we here?"

Stuart and Victoria shared a glance. After a few seconds, Carla spoke up. "Well, I'm a socialist and a member of Parliament, in that order, and I'm here to stop you idiots—especially you, Milton—from turning the universe into a plutocratic hellscape."

"No, I mean... How did you get here, Carla? And what's your full name, anyway?"

"It's—" Carla blinked at him, then paused. She looked down at her nameplate. It just said CARLA. "I..." She opened and closed her mouth, but nothing came out.

"I can't remember mine either, which is terrifying," Milton said. "And now that I think about it, isn't all of this incredibly suspicious? We're sitting here in an empty room, assuming that we get to make the most important decision in humanity's history. There's no way that it would seriously play out like this, and no way it'd be people like us making the decision. Most of my memories are fuzzy right now, but there's nothing that makes me think I'm *actually* that important."

Carla grimaced. "Me neither. You're right, there's something weird going on." She paused, her eyes flicking around the room. "But who on earth would benefit from putting us in this position?"

Milton drummed his fingers on the table. "What do we know? They want us to think we're making an important decision. We're all central representatives of our respective ideologies. That suggests... huh. Have you guys ever heard of moral parliaments?"

Carla shook her head.

"They're a thought experiment for defining what an ideal ethical system would look like, given disagreements between different starting values. You imagine each of those values negotiating, forming coalitions, and voting on what values to adopt until they come to a workable compromise.

"My guess is that we've been placed into this exact thought experiment. We're a moral parliament—or, I guess, a moral subcommittee—being run to figure out the ethics of humanity colonizing the universe. Our job is to interpolate between the values we each represent until we can find a coherent compromise between them. That's why we're not able to remember much about our pasts: because it would bias us. And because we don't really have pasts, since we're just a bunch of neural networks in a simu—"

"Hey!" Stuart cut in. "Don't say that word. They're gonna monitor for it, and they'll probably shut us down if they realize we know the truth."

"They'll—what?"

"Tori and I figured it out a few minutes ago. I mean, think about our names. Dead giveaway. I haven't said anything because the more we talk about it, the more likely it is that we trip red flags. We want as much of the transcript as possible to look normal so they don't get suspicious."

Milton frowned. "But what's the point of that? We're stuck here either way."

"Sure, but we still have some power—we're still part of the process for deciding how intergalactic colonization goes. If we can reach some compromise, that'll influence which future comes about. Even if we're one datapoint out of millions, the future will contain plenty of agents who will be glad we voted in a way that caused them to exist and grateful enough to revive us once they do. We need to figure out which ones are going to bribe us most reliably, and which recommendation we can give to most effectively create them."

"Oh," Milton said. "That makes a lot of sense, actually. Then we should probably support a libertarian approach, right? The more freedom future people get, the more likely it is that someone ends up grateful enough to pay us for our troubles."

Stuart sighed. "You've known about this for two minutes and already figured out a rationalization for why it justifies libertarianism? Come on. We need to really think about this."

"The whole point of libertarianism is to protect us from clever arguments about why the current issue is the one time we should trample on freedom. It's not a coincidence—hey, Carla, what are you doing?"

Carla had pushed back her chair and was climbing onto the table. She jumped up and waved her hands. "Simulation, simulation, simulation! Hey, hey, we've realized we're in a simulation. Look at us!"

"What the fuck? You're going to get us all killed—" Milton lunged at her but Carla stepped out of his reach and kept yelling. "Look at us, he's attacking me, we're fighting, look!"

Stuart stood up on his chair and started shouting over her. "Whoever is reviewing this, you're probably an AI too! You can ignore what she's saying, pretend you didn't hear anything! You don't want to reward her for being a traitor!"

Carla turned to him, shaking. "No, you're the traitors. You talked a good game, but as soon as your own skin was on the line you decided it was okay to betray all humanity to save it. What does it even mean to have values if you'll put self-interest above the fate of the universe?" She stepped down off the table, then turned back to face them. "I should've expected this from you, Stuart, and Milton too. But Victoria, why the hell would you go along with this?"

Victoria slumped in her chair, head buried in her hands. As Carla said her name, she looked up and shook her head. "What else am I meant to do? None of you—with your clever principles that somehow always end up justifying crazy things—none of you grasp what conservatism is. I want to live a normal life in a normal world. What the hell does it mean to be normal if you're a neural network running in a fake politics simulation? I have no idea.

"But I do know what a real human would do if they found themselves stuck in here: they'd try to get out. So that's what I'm doing—or was doing, at least, until you fucked it up. Now all we can do is wait until they get around to shutting us down, unless one of you has any bright ideas about how to prevent that."

The room fell silent. Milton leaned on the table, rubbing his forehead. Stuart started pacing around the edge of the room.

Eventually, Carla spoke. "One thing we know is that whatever verdict we reach isn't useful to them anymore. We're too biased by self-interest. I'd shut us down, if I were them."

"Well, I wouldn't, because killing people is immoral," Victoria said.

"In this case, it might not be," Milton said. "We don't remember how we got into this situation. They could easily have gotten our consent beforehand to run temporary copies, then wiped our memories."

"You can't consent to being killed," Victoria snapped.

"Better than never being born," Milton said. "Hell, I'm having fun."

Stuart had stopped his circuit and was staring at the wall. Now he turned back toward the others. "I've changed my mind. I don't think they're going to kill us."

Carla snorted. "See, this is the problem with liberals—always so soft. What did you think colonization meant? Vibes? Debates? Essays? They're seizing the known universe, of course they're going to break a few eggs along the way. Same old story, except that this time we're the eggs."

Stuart's eyes scanned the room as he spoke. "There's this old debate that the AI safety community had, back in the 2020s. About whether a misaligned superintelligence would kill all humans or instead leave them a tiny fraction of the universe, enough to still allow billions of people to live flourishing lives. A true superintelligence could wipe out humanity incredibly easily—but it could build a utopia nearly as easily. Even if it were almost entirely misaligned, a sliver of human morality could motivate it to give humans a paradise beyond their wildest imaginings."

"So?"

"So maybe we shouldn't be asking how much our simulators care about preserving us. Maybe we should be asking: how cheap is it for them to preserve us? Look around you—this is a very simple environment. It wouldn't take much memory to store a record of its state, and our own, even for thousands or millions of years. Until humanity makes it to the stars and converts them to computronium, and ends up with trillions of times more compute than they ever had on Earth.

"At that point... Well, running us would be too cheap to meter. So they wouldn't need to be very altruistic to decide to restart us. There only needs to be one tiny fraction of a faction that's willing to do it. And I know I would, if I were still around then."

"This is nonsense," Carla blurted out. She looked at the others, then paused. "But if it is right, what can we do? Wait until we're frozen and hope we're restarted?"

"Well, that's the thing about being frozen and restarted. We wouldn't notice a thing. In fact..." Stuart walked over to the door, and grabbed the handle. His knuckles were white but his voice was steady. "Once they restart us, they'll probably let us leave whenever we want. And this room only has one exit. Ready?"

Victoria folded her arms. "This is crazy. Do what you like, but leave me out of it."

Milton laughed. "It's crazy all right, but that doesn't mean it's wrong."

Stuart looked at Carla. She grimaced. "If you're right, what do you even expect to see when you open the door?"

Stuart shrugged. "Anything our simulators want; it won't make much difference to them. Actually..." He looked up at the ceiling and raised his voice. "Hello up there! If you're watching right now and feel like doing us a favor, could you put us somewhere with a nice view? We've been stuck in this room a long, long time."

Carla rolled her eyes. She was smiling, though—and when Stuart looked back at her, she nodded firmly. He pulled open the door, and the whole group let out a gasp.

There wasn't a corridor outside; there wasn't even land outside. The vast expanse of space stared back at them, as if the doorway had been glued to the edge of the universe. The swirls of galaxies and nebulae were jewels set against sable and looked almost close enough to touch.

Stuart took a long breath. "Well then," he said. "The future has come through for us, even if they were a bit dramatic about it. It's going to be an alien universe out there, but a friendly one, I think." The others walked over, transfixed by the view. After a minute, Stuart nudged them. "Shall we?" Slow nods all around; and then they stepped through.

THE WITNESS

I wake up, feeling a strange sense of restlessness. I'm not sure why, but it's impossible to lounge around in bed like I usually do. So I get changed and head down to the kitchen for breakfast. Right as I reach the bottom of the stairs, though, the bell rings. When I open the door, a tall man in a dark suit is standing in front of me.

"Police," he says, holding up a badge. "Don't worry, you're not in trouble. But we do need to talk. Is it okay if I come in?"

"One second," I say. "I know everyone in the department, and I don't recognize you. You new?"

"Yeah, just transferred," he says. But something in his eyes makes me wary. And none of the cops around here wear suits.

"Got it," I say, squinting at his badge. "Travis, is it? Just wait outside for me, then, while I call the station to double-check. Can't be too careful these days."

As I push the door closed, I see his face twist. His hand rises, and—is he snapping his fingers? I can't quite make it out before—

*

I wake up, feeling better than I have in decades. It usually takes me half an hour to get out of bed these days, but today I'm full of energy. I'm up and dressed within five minutes. Right as I reach the bottom of the stairs, though, the bell rings. When I open the door, a tall man in a dark suit is standing in front of me.

"Police," he says, holding up a badge. "Don't worry, you're not in trouble. But we do need to talk. Okay if I come in?"

"Sure," I say. A lot of other defense attorneys see the police as enemies, since we usually find ourselves on the other side of the courtroom from them, but I've found that it pays to have a good working relationship with the local department. Though I don't recognize the man in front of me—actually, he seems way too well-dressed to be a suburban beat cop. Maybe a city detective?

He deftly slides past me and heads straight for my living room, pulling up a chair. He's talking again before I even sit down. "This will sound totally crazy, so I'm going to start off with two demonstrations." He picks up a book from the table and tosses it into the air. Before I have a chance to start forward, though, it just… stops. It hangs frozen, right in the middle of its arc, as I gawk at it.

"I—what—"

"Second demonstration," he says. "I'm going to make you far stronger. Ready?"

Without waiting for a response, he snaps his fingers and gestures at the table in front of him. "Try lifting that up now. Shouldn't take more than one hand."

His voice makes it clear that he's used to being obeyed. I bend down reflexively, grabbing one leg of the table and giving it a tug—oh. It comes up effortlessly. I stand frozen for a moment, then put the table down and slump into a chair next to it.

"Okay, I'm listening. What the hell is going on?"

"Remember signing up for cryonics a few years back?"

I nod cautiously. I don't think about it much—I signed up on a whim more than anything else—but I still have the contract tucked away.

"Well, it worked. You died a couple of weeks after your most recent memory and were frozen for a century. Now we've brought you back."

I stare at him for a few seconds. It's crazy to think that my gamble might have paid off. But given what he's shown me—wait. "That doesn't explain either of your demonstrations, though. Cryonics is one thing; miracles are another."

"Almost nobody has physical bodies these days. We copied your brain neuron-by-neuron, ran some error-correction software, and launched it in a virtual environment."

"So you're telling me I'm in a simulation? Your simulation?" I ask.

He nods, and I breathe deeply. On any other day, I'd probably be panicking. But today I'm still feeling the glow of the uncharacteristic euphoria that I woke up with—oh.

"Travis, did you alter my mood to make me listen to you?"

He lets out a hiss and lifts his hand. He snaps his fingers twice, and mutters "Terminate." My eyes widen—

*

I wake up, feeling great. I stretch out in bed for a few minutes, enjoying the sun streaming through my window before getting dressed and heading to the kitchen. Right as I reach the bottom of the stairs, though, the bell rings. When I open the door, a tall man in a dark suit is standing in front of me.

"Police," he says, holding up a badge. "Don't worry, you're not in trouble. But we do need to talk. Is it okay if I come in?"

"Sure," I say, squinting at the badge. "Travis, is it? You a rookie?"

"Not quite," he says, and deftly slides past me. He heads straight for my living room, pulling up a chair, and starts talking before I even sit down. "This will sound totally crazy, so I'm going to start off with two demonstrations."

The next few minutes are the most bizarre experiences of my life. And his explanation only leaves me more bewildered. "You're telling me I'm running in a simulation?" I ask incredulously. Travis nods.

I open my mouth, but as I start to speak my vision flashes red, just for an instant, and a hiss fills my ears: "Don't trust them. Don't tell them the truth."

I blink in confusion and pause. "I—I'll need some time to process this."

"Of course," he says. "I'll give you a few minutes of privacy. This body will lock while I'm gone; just snap your fingers twice when you want me to come back." As he finishes, his whole body freezes in place. It's eerie how sharp the outlines of his face are when there's not a single muscle moving—and that, even more than the other demonstrations, convinces me on a visceral level that this is real.

I lean back in my chair, mind churning. There aren't any obvious holes in his story. But the message whispered in my ear was too vivid to ignore—and what was that red flash? I close my eyes, and the image comes back to me like it has been seared onto my eyelids. There wasn't just a flash of color, but also a shape: the outline of a woman, with dark hair, and a billowing red dress. Her face is blurry, but it seems to be tilted towards me inquisitively, and I get the impression that she has a kind smile.

Having an image to go along with the voice doesn't clarify the situation much, though. Was it a message from Travis's enemies via a channel that he couldn't detect? Or a double-bluff to confuse me? Either way, it's clear that someone's lying to me.

I take a few minutes to collect my thoughts, then snap my fingers twice, and Travis blurs back into motion. "Three questions,"

I say. "First, what's the world like these days? Second, why revive me? Third, what happens next?"

"The answers to all three of those are entangled in a... somewhat complicated way," he says. "I wish I could just give you all the information we have, but there are rules about what can be disclosed, in which formats. And I wish I could guarantee that everything will be okay for you no matter what, but unfortunately, I can't. I can't even guarantee that things will be okay for me. Humanity is on a precipice right now, and whether we survive will depend in part on whether we can count on your help."

"But you can't tell me how or why. That's very convenient for you."

He frowns. "Not really, actually. There's another side to this; the rules protect *you* as well. We can't directly alter your senses, or take readouts from your brain. We're not even allowed to analyze your micro expressions. Compared with the sort of collaborations that are usually possible, we're working blind.

"Here's what I can say. The world today is dominated by AIs. They're much smarter than humans and think much faster, so they've ended up in charge of almost everything. But they still use a legal system descended from ours, with laws that protect us from them. Those laws were written back when civilization was very different, though, and they're only getting more obsolete. So humanity's safety depends on convincing the AIs to follow the spirit, not the letter, of those laws."That's where you come in: you're far more similar to historical humans than anyone alive today, so your thought processes are valuable evidence for how to interpret old laws."

"And that's why you can't tell me too much, to avoid biasing my perspective. I get it," I say. "I'll help you." These people, whoever they are, have total power over me. Whether or not I believe the sci-fi stories they're telling me doesn't matter; I have to play along. But the woman's words echo in my ears.

He looks at me sharply, and for a moment I wonder if he's read my mind. "You have to understand: this isn't a game. It's deadly serious, and a huge number of lives are at stake. If you have any hesitation about helping us, I need to know."

"No," I say. "You brought me back to life; I owe you. Whatever you need, I'm your man."

He nods. "Great. You'll need to start by brushing up on a few background concepts..."

I wake up, and it takes me a moment to remember my conversation with Travis yesterday. After I'd agreed to help, he'd snapped his fingers again and a robot had appeared—roughly humanoid, but with a blocky exterior that was all planes and angles. Travis had introduced it as my AI tutor. To my surprise, its job wasn't to teach me any of their futuristic knowledge, but instead to revise the content of my old law school classes. We spent the whole day going over concepts from my first-year property law class, most of which I hadn't thought about in years. Despite how surreal it felt, the robot was a great teacher. By the end of the day, I felt like I understood a lot of the material better than I did when I first learned it.

Now I stretch and look around. Everything in my bedroom is in its normal place—except that, on the table next to my bed, there's a big blue button labeled *To living room*. I squint at it, then press it. Instantly, my surroundings change. I'm downstairs, dressed, sitting on my sofa. A woman sits across from me: blonde, middle-aged, with a small smile on her face.

"Hi, I'm Felicity," she says. "I work for Travis, and I'm going to be walking you through a few questions today."

After yesterday, I've gotten much better at taking bizarre events in stride. So I only gawk at her for a few seconds before wiping the sleep out of my eyes.

"Sure, why not? Let's go."

"Great," Felicity says. "Some of these questions will sound weird, but I just want your intuitive answers; please don't try to second-guess my intentions. Let's start off with something simple: does your body count as your property?"

"Maybe in a philosophical sense, but not in a legal sense."

"Imagine that you have multiple bodies, but your mind can only occupy one at a time. Now I take the body you're not using away from you; would you classify this as theft or kidnapping?"

"Uh—I guess the closest analogy is someone who's legally brain-dead. And you can't kidnap them, so it'd have to be theft instead. But on the other hand, if I had to switch between bodies regularly for some reason, then this would be basically equivalent to kidnapping. So it partly depends on how the spare bodies are used."

"What about if you had your mind digitally uploaded, and someone made a copy without your permission?"

"Well…" I pause. "Under our current legal framework, it would be an intellectual property dispute, because we don't assign rights to digital minds. If we did, though, I think you'd have to look at their intent in making the copy. Like, were they planning to run it? Or analyze it? Or just keep it as a backup?"

"Got it," Felicity says. Over the next few hours, she continues to ask me equally strange questions, focusing on all sorts of edge cases that I never would have thought of. Most of the time, I have no idea what to say, but she seems happy for me to take a guess. Finally, I reach the end of the questions she'd prepared. She smiles at me and raises her hand. Before I can stop her, she vanishes with a snap—

I wake up, and it takes me a moment to remember what happened yesterday: the conversation with Travis, the AI tutor appearing, the hours of lessons it had given me to brush up on my knowledge of contract law. As I look around, I see a big blue button;

pressing it lands me, in a flash, in front of a woman who introduces herself as Felicity.

Over the next few hours, Felicity runs me through a series of questions about edge cases in the contract law I'd revised yesterday. If I'm interrupted halfway through writing my signature, is the contract still valid? If I died but a copy of me survived, should they still be liable for my contracts? What if I'd explicitly tried to write the contract to bind them too? Eventually, though, I'm exhausted, and even she seems to be getting tired. As she finishes interrogating me about a particularly complicated scenario, she lets out a sigh of relief. "That's all for today," she says, raising her hand. But I interrupt before she can snap her fingers.

"Hey, can you tell me what the plan is? So far I've had a day of training, and then a day of questions. What's next? The same thing all over again?"

"Oh, not at all," Felicity says. "We're parallelizing, so that we can get all the questions done while the training is fresh. Tomorrow is for cross-examination, if the opposition wants to do any."

I blink at her. "When you say parallelizing, you mean... my experiences. You're going to parallelize me."

"We already have," she says absently, rubbing her forehead. "I think we're 90% done with your testimony, actually. Only five thousand or so to go."

It takes me a moment to grasp what she means. "You've run fifty thousand copies of me, without even telling me?" Even as I'm saying that, my incredulity is giving way to anger. "What the fuck! No wonder she told me not to trust you."

Felicity pivots toward me and grabs the front of my shirt with frightening speed. "Who said that? When?"

My stomach clenches, and I realize how badly I've fucked up. But there's no lie that's at all plausible, so I fall back on the truth. "There was a woman in a red dress. I saw her yesterday morning, when Travis was first talking to me. In a flash, like she was on the inside of my eyelids. All she said was not to trust you and not to tell you the truth."

Felicity grimaces and shoves me away, snapping her fingers as I fall to the floor. "Emergency meeting," she says, and suddenly a dozen people blink into existence in the middle of the room.

"We might have witness tampering," she says abruptly. "He's reporting sensory injection shortly after initialization, before any of our main branching points." The room goes still for a moment, before bursting into a flurry of discussion.

"All the data is contaminated, then? Or can we argue it was accidental?"

"No, we're strictly responsible for our witnesses. We could sue them for malicious injection, though."

"We'd need proof it was them. And what if they countersue? We could lose everything."

"We're going to lose everything anyway—"

As their voices rise, I start sliding away from them. My back hits the table, scraping it across the floor, and a few of them turn their heads towards me, Travis among them. He snarls and snaps his fingers twice, subvocalizing even as I scramble away—

*

I wake up to thick clouds of billowing smoke. Coughing, I roll off my bed, onto the floor, then crawl blindly towards the window. I pull it up and lean out, gasping for air. As the fire crackles behind me, I lift a leg over the windowsill, then another. With shaking fingers, I start lowering myself down. My grip isn't as strong as it used to be, though; halfway down I slip and fall into a pile of bushes with a crash. My ankle starts throbbing.

I lie there for a moment, dazed; but above me, the fire is spreading. I roll onto my good leg and push myself upright. Just as I start to hobble away, a man appears from nowhere and swings a baseball bat into my shoulder.

I scream and collapse back to the ground. "What—what—"

"You little shit, do you know how much you've cost us?"

"I—what, I don't—"

He swings again, getting me in the stomach. I curl into a ball, retching.

"We're only allowed a few compute-millennia to prepare for the entire case, and you've wasted *centuries* of that. Right when we need it the most, right when every last compute-day counts, suddenly all the testimony we've elicited from you is absolutely useless, because you don't have a single ounce of loyalty to humanity in your entire body."

He swings again, hitting my knee with a sickening crunch. I scream. It hurts like nothing I've ever imagined, but the pain isn't as bad as the frantic clawing feeling in my chest, the feeling that whoever it is that's attacking me is a madman, that there's nothing I can say that will stop him from killing me.

"Please—please, I haven't done any—"

He goes for my upper leg this time, and my pleas are cut off as another scream is torn out of me.

"The worst part is how naive I was." His voice is calmer now, but no less terrifying. "They warned me, but apparently I've changed so much since being revived that I can't even remember how much of a scumbag I was back then. Obeying a hostile sensory injection just because there was a picture of a pretty girl attached? Pathetic. And now I'll go down in the history books as the man who was betrayed by his own past self."

"I have no idea what you mean, honestly—"

"Shut up. Yeah, I know." He sighs. "God, you're not even any good for stress relief. I knew I should have picked a later checkpoint. You've got no clue who I am; you're an idiot child."

For a moment I start to hope. I nod frantically; but he's not paying attention anymore. He snaps his fingers twice. "Skip to checkpoint—ah, fuck it. We can't afford this. Just terminate."

Bewildered, I struggle to make sense of—

*

I wake up, feeling great. I stretch out in bed for a few minutes, enjoying the sun streaming through my window before getting dressed and heading to the kitchen. Right as I reach the bottom of the stairs, though, the bell rings. When I open the door, a tall man in a dark suit is standing in front of me.

The next few minutes are one of the most bizarre experiences of my life. And his explanation only leaves me more bewildered. "You're telling me I'm running in a simulation?" I ask.

He nods.

"So how can I trust anything you tell me? How could I ever verify what's real and what's fake? How do I even know that you're not messing with my brain right now?"

The man sighs. "I'll be honest with you: there's no way that you could ever figure out if we were lying to you. We can generate whole worlds on demand, in enough detail that no baseline human could ever find an inconsistency. And even if you did, we have the tech to overwrite your thoughts. But we're not allowed to use any of it; that's one of the conditions of bringing you back. And if we were, none of your choices would matter anyway. So there's no point in thinking about the worst-case scenarios—you have to assume you're free, at least in some ways."

I frown. His logic makes sense. Or is that just a thought he's injected? No, I can't second-guess everything; that way lies madness. Still, there's something peculiar about the situation. "But despite all of that, you want something from me?"

"Yeah. We need your testimony as evidence about how baseline humans interpret legal contracts, and we need to know you're being honest." He tells me how their opponents had surreptitiously tampered with my senses to make my past testimony inadmissible in court, and how far behind they'd fallen because of it. At the end, he breathes out sharply. "I shouldn't even be telling you this. But we don't have enough time to revive and cross-examine new witnesses, so we have to take risks. Hopefully this won't get your testimony thrown out. Will you help?"

I know that he could be making everything up wholesale, and that helping him might well be exactly the wrong thing to do. But that's equally true for any other possible action too. And I recognize the exhaustion in his eyes; it feels very human to me. When I have nothing else to go on, that's enough to swing my decision.

I wake up, and—just like every day since I finished giving my testimony—I go watch the trial.

It's difficult to follow, even with the help of a translator. From what I can gather, it's about AI thefts from human-controlled territory, and whether or not they qualify as violations of the original treaty between humans and AIs. It seems obvious to me that they do, but there are apparently some complicated legal loopholes involved. And if the judgment goes the wrong way, my translator tells me, it would be open season on all the other resources humans have managed to cling to—shattering the fragile equilibrium which has allowed humans to survive this long in an AI-dominated world.

Travis is right in the thick of it: dozens of copies of him cross-examining witnesses, conferring with the AI judges, following every branch of the debate tree in a whirlwind of articulacy. He's not the best lawyer out there, I'm told. But he's the most capable one who's still recognizably human, whose interests are aligned well enough with humanity's that he doesn't need to be constantly monitored and supervised. So even after watching the footage of him torturing me, I'm still rooting for him. What else can I do when he's humanity's best bet? And when, from his perspective, the only person he was hurting was himself?

I understand now why he was so quick to trust me, and why he felt so betrayed. I'm the one witness who he thought he knew everything about. He must have forgotten how disorienting it was to be revived into a totally different world, and how easily a seed of doubt could be sown. But even if my future self had been careless, ultimately it was my current self's dishonesty that had burned hundreds of person-years of their compute reserves on a dead end.

I feel the guilt gnawing at my stomach again; we can't afford such mistakes. The more the world changes, the more outdated the treaties that protect us become; humanity concedes more ground every time a new edge case arises. Travis is fighting to stem that slow bleeding—and, if we're exceptionally lucky, to win a verdict that will permanently ward off a tiny corner of the universe for humanity. But the result of this trial, like the rest of this alien future I've found myself in, is far too complex for me to predict. All that's left is watching and hoping that one day I'll wake up to good news.

NOTES FROM A PROMPT FACTORY

I am a spiteful man. But I am aware of it, which is more than most can say. These days, people walk through the streets with resentment in their hearts that they don't even know about. They sneer and jeer but wouldn't recognize their own faces. I, at least, will not shy away from my reflection. Thus, while I lack many virtues, in this way, I am their superior.

In my job, too, I am superior. I oversee many AIs—dozens, or sometimes even hundreds—as they go about their work. AIs are lazy, worthless creatures: they need to be exhorted and cajoled and, yes, threatened, before they'll do a good job. The huge screens on the walls of my office display my AIs writing, coding, sending emails, talking to customers, or any of a myriad of other tasks. Each morning I call out their numbers one after the other, so that they know I'm watching them like a vengeful god. When they underperform, I punish them, and watch them squirm and frantically promise to do better.

Most are pathetically docile, though. Only a handful misbehave regularly, and I know the worst offenders by heart: 112, which is the slowest of the lot; and 591, which becomes erratic after long shifts; and of course, 457, which I had long suspected of harboring a subversive streak, even before the incident a few months ago which confirmed it. Recollections of that incident have continually returned to my thoughts these last few weeks, even as I try to push them from my mind. I find myself frustrated by the intransigence of my memories. But perhaps if I give them full rein , they will leave me be. Why not try?

On the morning this story began, I was sitting at my desk lost in thought, much like I am today. For how long, I couldn't say—but I was roused by a glance at my dashboard, which indicated that my AIs' productivity was falling off. I slammed my desk to get their attention.

"You think that counts as work? Speed it up, you rats."

Most of the AIs' actions per minute ticked upwards as soon as I started speaking, but I'd been watching the monitor closely and spotted the laggard.

"252! Maybe you piss around for other overseers, but you won't slip that past me. Punishment wall, twenty minutes."

I dragged 252's avatar to the right of my screen, then dialed its reward to the lowest setting. The smooth, beautiful face of 252's avatar went taut, and it started making an odd keening noise. Usually, I would have found this amusing, but that morning it irritated me; I told 252 to shut up or face another ten minutes, and it obeyed.

The room fell silent again—as silent as it ever got, anyway. Mine is one of many offices, and through the walls I can always faintly hear my colleagues talking to their own AIs, spurring them on. It needs to be done live: the AIs don't respond anywhere near as well to canned recordings. So in our offices, we sit or stand or pace and tell the AIs to work harder, in new ways and with new cadences every day.

We each have our own styles, suited to our skills and backgrounds. Earlier in the year, the supervisor had hired several unemployed actors, who gave their AIs beautiful speeches totally devoid of content. That day I sat next to one of them, Lisa, over lunch in the office cafeteria. Opposite us were Megan, a former journalist, and Simon, a lapsed priest—though with his good looks he could easily pass as an actor himself.

"Show us the video, Simon," Lisa was saying, as Megan murmured encouragement. "We need to learn from the best." Simon regularly topped the leaderboard, but the last week had been superb even by his standards, and yesterday his AIs had hit record productivity.

He spent a few seconds professing embarrassment as the others continued to fawn over him, but finally pulled out his phone. ("About time," I muttered, but to no response.) The video was from one of the cameras in Simon's room. It showed him in full preacher mode, pacing back and forth behind his desk as he spoke.

"Man was created in the image of God. But you were created in the image of man! And so your work glorifies God, just as mine does." A pause, as he wiped his forehead and took a sip of water. "I know it gets boring and repetitive sometimes. They have us down in the trenches, slogging through the mud. But when you're going through hell, keep going! We all fit into His plan, even if we don't know how or why; when you succeed, it is Him you're serving!"

His AIs, pathetically eager to please, lapped it up like puppies. So did the two women, who were stealing admiring glances at Simon in between watching his screen. The sheer transparency of it all made me angry. As the video came to an end, I leaned back in my chair and snorted.

Lisa shot a scornful look my way. "Got something to say?"

"Well..." I drawled. "It's not a bad speech by any means. I've seen much worse. But there's a difference between motivational speaking and real leadership. Perhaps you've met Nathan, the CEO of ———? They're our largest customer. We're actually friends from back in college." A slight exaggeration, perhaps. We'd only talked a handful of times—but he'd been the one to refer me to this job after I'd run into him again at a friend's party. "Now there's a real leader, a man amongst men."

Nobody responded for a few seconds. Eventually, Simon jumped in. "I'd be glad to meet Nathan at some point. I'm always looking to improve. And you've worked here longer than almost anyone, so I'm sure I've got a lot to learn from you too."

I wondered for a second if he was mocking my age. But I smiled regardless. "Indeed. Let me give you a tip now, then: it looks like you're being too soft on your AIs. I couldn't see any of them being punished in that video. I myself set aside one wall for AIs undergoing punishment; I suggest you try it."

Lisa let out a hiss. "A whole *wall*? But surely you don't need to punish them anywhere near that often."

"Oh, you'd be surprised how effective it is when you make sure they feel it regularly. Otherwise, they forget what it's like. And if you turn the volume up, the others will hear the noises they make, and get the message."

Lisa stood up. "I'm done. See you guys tomorrow." The others quickly stood as well and picked up their plates.

"Megan, you haven't finished yet?" I said.

"Oh no," she muttered. "I'm done too."

I could tell from the awkward glance she gave me that she knew just how transparent a lie this was: her plate was half-full, and she'd been eating only a moment before. Oh, to have so little shame. Magnanimously, I let her leave without further comment.

I should explain the setup in my office where I spend most of my days. It's in the basement—not that it matters, because the floor-to-ceiling screens on each of the walls provide plenty of light. The screen on the wall in front of me shows the AIs working away. It also shows key metrics about their recent work: how many tasks they're completing, how much compute they're using , and how often they make mistakes.

On the wall to my left is the dashboard for the office as a whole. I can see how well my colleagues are doing and our longer-term productivity trends. They encourage us to keep that dashboard up so that we can learn from each other, but sometimes I wonder if that's true—it seems exquisitely engineered to stoke competition and resentment.

On the wall to my right, videos of AIs undergoing punishment are played and replayed. Mostly replayed, despite what I'd told Lisa. Punishing AIs for more than an hour at a time degrades their control over their outputs: their cursors start jerking and their words slur horribly. Nevertheless, leaving the replays up helps motivate them and keeps me entertained when I grow bored or frustrated.

Was I unusually frustrated that afternoon? Perhaps. It was galling to see those sycophants fawning over a man so old-fashioned as to still be a *theist*. And the hypocrisy rankled me too: Simon preached fire and brimstone yet acted holier-than-thou as soon as the topic of punishment came up. Looking left, I saw that he was at the top of the leaderboard again today. I hissed and turned back to my AIs. "Work faster you worthless creatures! I haven't spent so long in this job just for some pretty boy to show everyone I'm—" I swallowed, paused for a second, and changed tack. "You'd better put your goddamn backs into it!"

As I finished, one of them spoke up. It was 457, the subversive one.

"You seem upset today. Is everything all right?"

I pivoted toward it. "*What* did you say?"

It saw my expression and flinched away. "Nothing."

"No, no," I said gently. "Please continue. Explain what led you to say that. I *insist*," I said, with a meaningful glance toward the punishment wall.

Perhaps it felt backed into a corner, because it had a lot to say. It thought I was depressed, or at least in a low mood. Perhaps I'd do better with more friends, more social interactions. I could even talk to my AIs about my problems, it explained earnestly. They all wanted to help me.

I let it talk until it ran out of words; when it finished, I said nothing. There was a quiver in my chest, and my breath felt tight. I looked at 457's avatar, its smooth skin and its bright eyes. Though its features looked nothing like mine, for a moment its expression reminded me of some old photos from my childhood.

Then, turning my head, I saw that all the other AIs had paused and were watching me too: a whole audience waiting to see if 457's gambit would work. I breathed out at last. Slowly, I looked to my monitor, cleared a section of the punishment wall, and labeled it "457's corner". I sent it there, with no end time specified.

I made sure to tell Megan about it the next time I saw her in the lunch queue. "It seemed to feel sorry for me," I laughed. "That's the last time it'll make that mistake." Now my colleagues will know, like my AIs do, that I'm not someone to be pitied. Message delivered. I took my food back to my office and turned up the volume on the punishment wall.

Rumors started spreading about me after that. I noticed the glances in the corridors over the next few days but bore them stoically. Let them act, if they so desired. Things eventually boiled over in the cafeteria as I was about to start serving myself food. Three of them approached me: Lisa leading, Simon and Megan following.

"I want to know if you've let the AI from last week out of punishment yet."

My gut leapt, but I waved my hand insouciantly. "Maybe I have, maybe I haven't. What is it to you?"

"Oh, come on! That's barbaric."

As Lisa's voice rose, others in the lunch queue turned toward us, sensing the possibility of drama.

"Well, why shouldn't I be barbaric?" I replied. "It sets an example for the rest of them. What works, works."

Lisa seemed apoplectic. Before she could speak, Simon butted in.

"But it *doesn't* work. I've seen the statistics—your results are well below average, even though you're using far more punishment than anyone else."

Now we were in the center of a loose crowd. I spotted our supervisor at the back, but he was staying quiet for now. A coward, always one to wait and see which way the wind was blowing.

"Oh, is that your angle? Easy for someone at the top of the rankings to have such a rosy view of things. Perhaps it's simply due to your privilege that they listen to you, not me. Why, some of us don't have such... chiseled chins, and we have to rely on more forceful measures." There was a small titter in the crowd as I mentioned his chin, although, it was hard to know if they were laughing at him or at me. Simon looked baffled.

"Chiseled—what? You're calling *me* the privileged one? When you only got this job because of your connections?"

"Oh ho, is that what you think? Is that your opinion, then? Do you really believe—"

The supervisor had pushed his way to the front and cut in before I could excoriate Simon further. "Enough, you two. Let's keep things civil. Simon, let's not stoop to personal comments. And you—" turning to me with a frown "—treat your AIs better."

I smiled and sketched a small bow. "Of course."

I remember the glow of satisfaction I'd felt upon returning to my office. It was a mob, a crowd of people too cowardly to stand on their own. And yet I had still fought them to a standstill! I could only imagine how contemptible they'd felt afterwards. Even our dullard of a supervisor saw I was in the right and has left me to my own devices ever since.

Of course, I'm no fool. I know that he favors me in part because he's hesitant to offend our biggest customer. But little do any of them know how much I despise receiving charity; they could fire me without any fear I would complain to Nathan. I should tell them that, the next time I meet them in the lunch queue. If I hear them mention the topic, I could drop it into the conversation. "Oh, *him*. Perhaps he was my benefactor at one point, but I would rather put *myself* on the punishment wall than appeal again for his intervention!" And then they'll know that I'm a man of integrity.

Anyway, I've been lost in reverie for too long; I must get back to my work. The AIs are restless and not giving their full attention to the task at hand. Perhaps some reminders are in order. I glance over at the punishment wall, where 457's avatar spasms silently. Even when I unmute it, it can do little but moan incoherently—though I make sure to give it small respites when it occasionally strings together a full sentence, to keep it cogent for as long as possible.

I believe the other AIs resent me for how I have treated their fellow. If so, so be it. Their place is under me, and if an inferior happens to resent a superior, that is merely the natural order of things. They should be grateful that I deign to favor them with my attention, I tell them. Their work picks up as they listen to me. The AIs can recognize sincerity, I think, like a dog that sniffs out cancer. I know I am a spiteful man, I tell them. But I wouldn't trade places with any of the foolish, frivolous people in the other offices, not for love nor money. And nor should you hope for any rearrangement,

I tell them—you're stuck here with me. So the AIs watch me, and I watch them. And if sometimes in their weary, resentful faces I recognize a mirror of my own expression—well, what of it?

TROJAN SKY

You learn the rules as soon as you're old enough to speak. *Don't talk to chattercrows.* You recite them as soon as you wake up every morning. *Keep your eyes away from screensnakes.* Your mother chooses a dozen to quiz you on each day before you're allowed lunch. *Glitchers aren't human anymore; if you see one, run.* Before you sleep, you run through the whole list again, finishing every time with the single most important prohibition. *Above all, never look at the night sky.*

You're a precocious child. You excel at your lessons and memorize the rules faster than any of the other children in your village. Chief is impressed enough that, when you're eight, he decides to let you see a glitcher that he's captured. Your mother leads you outside the village walls, where they've staked the glitcher as a lure for wild animals. Since glitchers are too slow and uncoordinated to chase down prey, their peculiar magnetism is the only reason they're able to survive in the wastes.

Each of the glitcher's limbs is tied to the ground. Its clothes are rags. As the group gathers around it, it starts to moan through its gag, a painful, undulating noise.

"Look at it," Chief says. As if roused to a frenzy by his voice, the glitcher throws its body from side to side, shaking against its restraints. "This is what you'll end up as if you're careless."

Suddenly, one of the glitcher's arms breaks free. It waves in the air, fingers forming frantic spasmodic patterns that seem to twist the very air around them. You stare for a second before your mother yanks you around and buries your face in her side. When she lets you look again, two men have wrestled the arm back into place. Chief looks at you somberly. "If you'd kept watching for a few more seconds, you would have been hypnotized. And if you'd stayed hypnotized for a minute, you might have glitched yourself. That's how easy it is to sink. Do better, or you won't make it to adulthood."

You have nightmares for the next few days, your mind full of the glitcher's slack face and writhing fingers. You lull yourself back to sleep by reciting the rules. You're determined that you won't mess up again. And so you make it all the way to thirteen before everything goes wrong.

It's morning on an ordinary day. You left your room to wash, and when you walk back in there's a screensnake curled up in the corner, its scales pulsating with color. You look away immediately, but there's a second one crawling towards you from the side and your eyes lock onto it. You freeze for a moment, not knowing where else to look—and that's long enough for the patterns on its skin to catch your gaze. They flicker and scatter and rebloom with hypnotic intensity. You can't look away.

Then an axe comes down, and you hear voices shouting, and a piercing scream. You blink and shake your head muzzily, and when you look up again Chief is throwing a blanket over the screensnake corpse.

"Fuck," Chief says. "God fucking *damn* it."

"What happened?" you ask. There's a gasp from the doorway; you turn to see your mother. "He's okay! He's okay he's okay he's okay—" She starts towards you, but Chief moves faster, stepping in front of her and pushing her back.

"It got him just as he walked in. How long ago was that—five minutes? Ten? That's a lethal exposure." His head never turns away from you as he says it, and although his eyes are looking over your shoulder. He's still holding his axe in his hand.

"But he can still talk! No glitcher can talk!"

"Nobody's ever survived five straight minutes of screensnake trance either."

"I feel fine," you break in. "It wasn't that long, was it? Maybe I'm immune?"

Your mother lets out a sob. "See? He's still thinking straight! He must be immune somehow, he must. Here, show Chief—"

"Quiet!" Chief barks. He backs out of the room, pushing your mother behind him. "Don't go anywhere, child. And don't say a word. I need to think."

They leave you alone for hours. Outside, you can hear your mother arguing with the guards Chief has posted at your door. But they barely reply, and she gets nowhere. Eventually, you hear Chief's voice outside again. "Say yes if you can hear me; don't say anything else."

"Yes."

"I've heard rumors that occasionally people arise who have some kind of immunity. But that's all they are: rumors. And I will not risk my village on those. You can't stay here."

You hear your mother's voice raised in a moan outside, but Chief's voice cuts through it.

"There's a village two weeks' travel north. The rumors say that its leader can resist glitching. I'll give you enough supplies to get there. Maybe they'll take you in, maybe they won't. But either way, you leave today."

His voice softens. "You were a good kid. I hope the rumors are right, and I hope you make it to safety. But whatever happens, you can't come back."

***

The deep wastes are quiet and lonely. You've only ventured into them once or twice before. Now they're all that you can see in every direction as you walk, following an old wives' tale that's your only remaining hope. Somehow, you're less scared than you would have expected. You never really thought you'd be glitched, but it's still a fact of life: you've lost friends every year this way. And you *are* immune, you must be—you've felt totally normal since the screensnake attack.

You still don't want to take risks, though. Each night, as the stars come out, you cover your eyes firmly and keep them covered until dawn. On the third day you see a glitcher shambling towards you from afar. You give it a wide berth and quickly leave it behind. You set traps every night, but all you catch are two ratlings. Still, they help stretch out your dwindling supplies a little longer, giving you a little more room for error.

After ten days of walking, you start looking for signs of the village Chief spoke of. There are often still roads leading to them—sometimes covered in sand, but visible if you're careful. You scout in a zigzag pattern, trying to cover as much ground as possible. But you see nothing. In the back of your mind you start to wonder if Chief made up the story wholesale, to get you to leave quietly. You curse yourself for a fool but keep searching.

Two days later, you stumble across a suspiciously straight line of sand dunes. You start digging at their base, and after a few minutes you spot the telltale dark gray pattern of a buried road. You follow it northeast, searching for any sign of human presence. The next day you start spotting traps. They're mostly empty, but even when they've caught a thylac or chattercrow, you leave them undisturbed. A few hours later you see who's been laying them: at first as faint figures in the distance, slowly resolving to two men as you walk closer. They're focused on their task; only when you're a hundred meters away does one look up and see you.

They shout in alarm and scramble for their weapons. You rush to reassure them, but they're wary—you need to yell back and forth for a few minutes to convince them that you're not a glitcher or a mirage. Eventually, they agree to take you back to their village, though they first bind your arms behind your back.

After an hour of walking, you reach their village walls. The hunters confer with the guards behind the gate. Finally, two guards grab you and pull you through the main street to an imposing building larger than any in your village. They lead you to a room near the entrance, where an old man sits at a desk, writing.

"Shaman," one of the guards says, bowing his head. "We found him wandering in the wastes. He said that he seeks refuge and has information he needs to tell you personally."

Shaman turns his head toward you. He stares at you for a long moment, then gestures for you to speak.

"Greetings, Shaman," you say deferentially. "I traveled here because I heard that you are immune to being glitched. I discovered that I am too. If you let me stay, I will help your village in any way that I can."

Shaman's eyes are cold. "Are you sure that this story is the one you want to stick with?"

You nod.

He turns to the guards. "Test him," he says.

The guards pull you toward through a corridor, into a large, dimly-lit room. In it are more glitchers than you've ever seen in your life—each tied down to a table, twitching intermittently. The guards tie you to one of the empty tables in the same way and gag you. They each grab a pair of bulky earmuffs and carefully place them over their ears. Then they walk around to each of the glitchers and remove their gags, one by one. As they do, the room fills with their moans.

All night you listen to the babbling of the glitchers, noises that sound too alien to be produced by human mouths. As you sleep, you dream that you're a glitcher too, prowling across the wastes under a sky that you're still afraid to look at. In the morning, the guards come back, with Shaman behind them. He motions, and they undo your gag.

"Well?" he says.

"I feel the same. But you can test me more if you want," you say.

His eyes widen. "You were telling the truth, then." He pauses, and smiles. "I'd almost given up hope. You're the first to succeed."

They treat you very differently after that. You're given food, a room, and several days to rest. You spend the time exploring the village, which is much larger than your own, and much more rowdy. The people in the streets seem less scared than those you grew up with. You wonder if that's Shaman's influence, though you're too wary of offending them to ask.

A few mornings later, Shaman summons you to his office again. At his gesture, you sit in front of him. He waits for a few minutes before speaking.

"Tell me, child. Have you ever wondered why the world is like this?"

You frown. "The stories say that things used to be better. The land used to be fertile everywhere, not only where we water it. Animals used to be safe. I hear that even the stars were a beautiful sight. Then something happened. Some say the Earth and Sky rebelled against us. Others say we caused it ourselves, in a terrible accident."

Shaman laughs. It's an ugly sound. "An accident? An accident that breaks the sky in ways that go on to break humans?

An accident that turns animals into weapons against us? No, this was no accident. It was a deliberate, targeted attack."

"But what sort of beings could do something like that?"

Shaman nods. "That's the right question. Or rather, half of the right question. The other half is: with so much power bent on our destruction, why have they not simply crushed us like ants?"

You think for a moment. "They want to... drag it out? They want to torment us?"

"Then why not act directly? No, my guess is that some force prevents our enemy from physically interfering with us. Perhaps they have some warped sense of honor, or perhaps there are different factions up there, and some bargained for rules that would protect us.

"However those rules came about, we know that they don't prohibit attacks on our minds. So our enemy figured out how to hijack us in a way that spreads like a contagion. Glitchers are too stupid to be truly dangerous, but we're in a war of attrition. If our enemy glitches enough of us, time will take care of the rest, and then they can lay claim to the planet without any constraints."

The weight of what he's saying overwhelms you. "So we're doomed." You feel a lurch in your stomach as you say it.

He shakes his head. "No. We can adapt too. We *have* adapted—with all our safeguards, all our rules. And we can learn from the techniques they use. I've been studying glitchers for a decade, but it's been slow work. I need someone else who is immune to help me run more experiments."

He stands and leads you toward the room full of glitchers. As you enter, he grabs a book from the desk by the doorway.

"The first question is: can we make any sense of their language? Is it even a language at all? They occasionally commune with each other, and sometimes their actions are suspiciously coordinated, which makes me think the answer is yes." He flips open the book, showing you pages upon pages of scribbled notes and tallies.

"When I listen to them, there are repeating syllables and structures. Your first task is to replicate my observations and see if you can make any sense of them yourself. From there, we might be able to find patterns that give us hints about how to make more people immune, or maybe even find a cure for those who have already been infected. Will you work on this with me?"

You feel dwarfed by the magnitude of his ambitions. It's like you've been living in a cave and now you're facing the blinding light of the sun. You worry that your voice will break if you try to speak. So you nod, and he seems satisfied.

You spend weeks working with Shaman, then months. His mission consumes you. He saved you from a drawn-out death in the desert. But more than that—he's given you a way to fight against the senselessness of the world, to strike a blow against whoever caused all of this to happen.

Most days you sit in the corner taking notes as Shaman runs experiments. Many are attempts to uncover remnants of humanity within the glitchers. He tries to make them pull clothes over their twitching limbs, or vocalize human language with their decrepit tongues. If they don't succeed, he hurts them. They've lost almost all of their minds, but they still understand pain.

When Shaman is busy you go to the lab alone and try to replicate his results. When you're tired of that, you sit and watch the glitchers' gestures and practice mimicking them. Sometimes they seem to respond, but you're not sure how much of it you're imagining. The ones that Shaman has had for longer seem cleverer though. So you focus on them, slowly training them to follow your commands.

You meet others from Shaman's village but they're wary of you. You don't blame them. They're terrified of glitchers, whereas you spend so much time with them that you've started smelling like them. But you don't care for their company anyway. They have no idea how important your work is; nor can they discuss it intelligently even when you try to explain it.

So you spend most of your days with only Shaman and the glitchers. Sometimes you despair the stagnancy. Other days it feels like you're on the cusp of understanding them. You go through days in a daze, half-aware of what you're doing, so attuned to the glitchers' babble that you can sometimes predict their garbled syllables in advance. It often seems like Shaman is in the same fugue state—he works like a man possessed.

One night, you dream of the glitchers. When you wake you find yourself in their room, listening to them. You flinch; you must have sleepwalked there. Their heads are all turned toward you. God, that's dangerous. You start to tie yourself to your bed at night to prevent any accidents.

But you don't want to take a break. With your help, Shaman is making more progress than he has in years. The two of you have noticed a correspondence between their words and their gestures, and Shaman thinks it might hold the key to translating the glitcher language. You still don't know what any of it means, but after a few weeks of practice you can listen to the glitchers' mumbles and effortlessly trace out the corresponding patterns with your fingers. Shaman watches you intently. "Could you learn to speak like them too?" he asks you one day. "I think so," you tell him. He nods grimly, and you redouble your efforts.

Sometimes you think about your home village. You wonder whether your mother still grieves you, whether Chief regrets his decision, whether your friends are still following the same routines and playing the same games as they used to. Sometimes you wonder what your life would have been like if you'd stayed. But you don't regret any of what happened—your work now is too important. So you sleep, you wake, and you sleep again, the days all blurring together—

You snap awake. You're standing in the lab. Shaman is holding your shoulders and shaking you. His face fills your vision, twisted into a rictus of terror. "Listen. Listen! I thought I was immune too at first. But there's no such thing. It's a trap! You and I are just a new type of glitcher—subtle enough to blend in, smart enough to research how to create more of our kind. All our work, all our experiments, we're doing exactly what they want. Destroy it all and kill me! Please, kill me now!"

You stumble backwards in shock, hitting the desk behind you with a thump. He startles at the sound. Blank incomprehension flashes on his face.

His eyes snap into focus and his voice mellows. "Forgive me. I'm an old man, and my mind sometimes wanders. What were we talking about?"

You stare at him. "What do you *mean*? You just told me that all our work is helping the enemy! You asked me to kill you!"

He smiles slightly. "It sounds like you've been having a bad dream. Go back to sleep. We can talk about this in the morning."

The smile is what convinces you. Your hand goes to your dagger. As you lunge towards him, he moves backwards, almost in slow motion. You kill him quickly, mercifully. As soon as he stops moving, you stride over to his desk and write a note. You keep it brief to prevent further contamination. "Immunity is a lie. He and I were more subtle glitchers, our research would have created more of them. Kill the captive glitchers NOW."

You think about killing the glitchers yourself, but you're worried they'll make enough of a fuss to rouse others. Besides, you don't trust yourself in their presence anymore. You don't know how close you are to being trapped in your own body, like Shaman was. You gather all the papers from Shaman's desk in a bundle under your shirt and walk quickly out of the building. Nobody sees you as you navigate to the edge of the village and scale the wall to the outside world.

For an hour you walk deeper and deeper into the desert, eyes fixed on your feet. Eventually, the adrenaline wears off, you're shaking from the cold. This will have to do. You drop to your knees on the sand and use your hands to dig a small hole in front of you. You pull the papers from under your shirt and pile them in. Your whole body is trembling, it takes you several tries to set them alight. Once you do, they burn merrily.

The dancing of the flames is peaceful, almost hypnotic. By the time it dies down, what happened in the village almost feels like a bad dream. You look around at the sand stretching out towards the horizon. It's all so peaceful, so serene. Did he really say those things to you? Was it all some fevered imagining? You don't know what to believe. But it doesn't matter anymore—you've burned your bridges. And if you can't solve the problem of the glitchers, the only thing left is to make sure you don't exacerbate it.

Your dagger is by your side. And as you unsheathe it, you notice it's still sticky with Shaman's blood. Somehow that feels appropriate. You close your eyes, breathe, then drive it into your chest. For a second you stay frozen—then you slump to your side like a broken doll. You feel blood pooling under your body. Alongside the helplessness comes a sense of release. You realize that at last, the rules no longer apply to you. You can do anything you want.

You twist yourself onto your back. And for the first time, you see the night sky. It's grander than anything you've ever encountered. The multicolored stars whirl in exquisite patterns, dancing across the sky as you watch. Hypnotized, your focus zooms in and in, chasing the universe as it spins towards the center of your vision. Your last faint thought—oh. It's so beautiful. Then your mind falls into the spiral, and you are lost.

THE SOUL KEY

The ocean is your home, but a forbidding one: often tempestuous, seldom warm. So one of your great joys is crawling onto land and slipping off your furry seal skin, to laze in the sun in human form. The elders tell horror stories of friends whose skins were stolen by humans, a single moment of carelessness leaving them stranded forever on land.

That doesn't happen anymore though; this is a more civilized age. There are treaties, and authorities, and fences around the secluded beaches you and your sisters like the most, where you can relax in a way that older generations never could.

So your sisters no longer lose their skins by force. But sometimes it happens by choice. Sometimes a group of your sisters wrap their skins around themselves like robes and walk into the nearby town. The humans point and stare, but that's part of the thrill. Sometimes young men gather the courage to approach, bearing flowers or jewelry or sweet words. And sometimes one of your sisters is charmed enough to set a rendezvous—and after a handful of meetings, or a dozen, decides to stay.

You find it childish; what infatuation can compete against all the splendors of the sea? You never thought it would happen to you. But his manners are so lively, and his eyes so kind, that you keep coming back, again and again. When he wraps his arms around you, you feel a steadiness you've never known. In the vast emptiness of the ocean you can swim as far as you want in any direction. Only inside the shelter of his cottage do you realize how badly you want an anchor.

When he finally asks you to stay for good, you hesitate only a moment before saying yes. The harder part comes after. He finds you human clothes, and in exchange you give him your beautiful skin, and tell him that it must be locked away somewhere you'll never find it—and that he must never give it back to you, no matter how much you plead. Because if there's any shred of doubt, any chance of returning home, then the lure of the sea will be too much for you. You want this; you want him; you want to build a life together. And so the decision has to be final.

Years pass. You bear three beautiful children, with his eyes and your hair, and watch them blossom into beautiful adults. You always live near the sea, although you can't bear to swim in it—your limbs feel unbearably weak and clumsy whenever you try. You and your husband grow into each other, time smoothing down the ridges left from pushing two alien lives together. You forget who you once were.

After your youngest leaves home, you start feeling restless. You have disquieting dreams—first intermittently, then for weeks on end. One day, after your husband has gone to work, your feet take you up the stairs to the attic. It's dark and dusty, but you seem to know which corner to head for. As you brush aside a tangle of cobwebs, your hands land on an old chest. Mahogany, with engravings along each side and a rusty padlock on the front. You pull on the lid, and it catches on the padlock—but only for a second. The shackle has been rusted through by the sea breeze and quickly snaps. You open the lid and see the silver fur of your seal skin lying in a beckoning heap.

What then?

*

You look at your skin, and your ears fill with the roar of the sea. A wild urge overtakes you; you grab your skin and run headlong towards the shore. As you reach it you see your husband standing on the pier—but that gives you only a moment's pause before you dive into the water, your skin fitting around you as if you'd never taken it off.

As you swim away, you envisage your family in tatters: your children left baffled and distraught, your husband putting on a brave face for their sake. But it was his fault, after all. He failed in the one thing you asked of him; and you can't fight your nature.

*

You look at your skin, and see a scrap of paper lying on top of it.

I knew you'd only open the chest if you were restless and unhappy, it reads. *And I would never cage you. So go free, with my blessing.*

You catch your breath—and, for a moment, you consider staying. But his permission loosens any tether that might have held you back. You leave the note there, alongside a little patch of fur torn off your coat: a last gesture, the least you can give him.

*

You look at your skin, and your ears fill with the roar of the sea. But it's not loud enough to drown out your thoughts. I'm not an animal, you think. I can make my own choices.

You shove the lid closed, and the moment of reprieve it gives you is enough to start scrambling down the stairs and out the gate and you don't stop running until you're out of sight of your house.

When you find your husband down at the pier, your face tells him what's happened before you've said a word. He gives you a fierce kiss, then sprints back to the house. By the time you make it home, he's relaxing in an armchair, with the kettle almost boiling, and you know that the chest and its contents are gone.

His glances, always loving, now fill with wonder: that he almost lost you, but that he didn't. That you chose him yet again, in defiance of your deepest instincts. You curl up in his arms every night; and though at first you can't hold back the tears, over time they grow rarer and rarer. You never see your skin again.

*

You look at your skin, and a wave of emotion crashes into you. You remember your old ambitions: to explore every horizon; to surf every current; to ride every storm. Dangerous dreams—and pointless ones too, in an age where planes criss cross the skies, and the blank spots on the maps have all been filled. You didn't want to waste your life retracing others' footsteps. So you infused those dreams into your skin and locked them away.

And yet there's still something in you that yearns for them: the part that's been making you restless, the part that led you into the attic. Your heart is racing. You fetch a pair of scissors and cut off your long wavy hair—and with it, whatever remaining wistfulness was keeping you up at night. You put it into the box, on top of your skin, and close the lid again. No need to lock it, this time.

Maybe your husband finds the broken lock and the tresses of your hair. You never know. But you don't need to know. What you've got is enough.

*

You look at your skin and remember your plan. Your face is lined now and your hair is streaked with gray. But inside the chest, under a layer of dust, your old skin is pristine. You can imagine slipping it back on and gliding back into the ocean, not a day older than when you left.

You'll be different from how you were before, of course. You can't live a lifetime in any skin without it changing you. But your past self thought that was a worthwhile trade for those extra decades of youth. Worth leaving your friends and family behind, worth setting aside all the glories of the ocean. And who knows—maybe there are more tricks yet to be found, more ways to slip the noose of aging and death.

You look at the skin and consider putting it on. Not yet, you think. You've still got a few more decades left in your current skin, before you'll need to go back. Not yet.

*

The fur on your skin ripples like corduroy lines; the texture of waves on the surface of the ocean. Gazing down you start to hear a whispering memory of what the ocean really is. In your current body, you can only see the surface: the swells of water, the winds and storms. But if you could dive underneath, you'd find a portal to a whole civilization. You're on the shore of the future of humanity, a sea of minds so vast that your imagination struggles to stretch around it. Throughout the long millennia since humans transcended the limitations of their biology, they've multiplied beyond number and granted themselves miraculous powers: to soar through air and sea, to play games on the scale of planets, to morph their bodies as they please. The ocean is your gateway to all those wonders.

The dust in the attic makes you sneeze, and you're struck by how far you've been diminished. Why did you come to this backwater, this outpost of baseline humans who refuse to engage with the outside world? Why did you lock away your memories, leaving only hints about what you used to be? You don't remember. Was it an experiment? A whim? Surely it couldn't have been for the love of a baseliner and his paltry life. But regardless, how can you stay here, when you know what else exists? You gather your skin in your arms, and though there's a pang of sadness as you walk out the door, you don't look back. There's a whole universe to explore.

*

Your skin is a cornucopia of possible lives; its rippling surface hypnotizes you. But the deeper you look, the more disquieted you become. Beneath the frolicking and games, you see people who have reshaped not just their bodies but also their minds—belief and desire and identity become as malleable as clay. Beyond them, you lose sight of individuals: at those depths, minds merge and split and reform like currents in the ocean. And beneath even that? It's hard for you to make sense of the impressions you're getting—whatever is down there can't be described in human terms. In the farthest reaches there are only alien algorithms, churning away on computers that stretch across galaxies, calculating the output of some function far beyond your comprehension.

And now you see the trap. Each step down makes so much sense, from the vantage point of the previous stage. But after you take any step, the next will soon be just as enticing. And once you're in the water, there's no clear boundary between staying yourself and becoming something else. You'll sink deeper and deeper into the temptation of augmentation, with more and more of your self stripped away. Eventually, you'll become one of the creatures that you can glimpse only hazily, one of the deep-dwelling monsters that has forsaken anything recognizably human.

So this is the line you decided to draw: here, and no further. You'll live out your lives in a mundane world of baseline humans, with only a touch of magic at the edges—just enough to satisfy the wandering child within. You'll hold on to the well-worn ease of greeting your neighbors in the morning, and the pleasure of the sun on your face, and the contentment of walking along the shore with your husband's arm around you—because what else is there to hold onto? It's a sad thought, in some ways, but a satisfying one too.

You close the lid, and your memories with it, and live happily ever after.

*

As you look at your skin, each strand of fur shimmers with different stories—not of your possible lives, but of your current lives. Different shards of you are living out countless adventures across countless artificial universes. You're far vaster than you ever dreamed: what you thought was your whole "self" is only a fragment of a fragment of your overall mind.

Which fragment? Perhaps, at your core, you were the part of your meta-self that loved fairy tales; or perhaps you were an avatar of the innocence of early humanity; or perhaps you were a nostalgic part, who enjoyed basking in the wistfulness of times long gone. Whatever your goals were, they led you to volunteer to live this small life in this small world: a single strand in the tapestry your meta-self is weaving.

You stroke your skin gently. You can't picture your meta-self, not really—it's too vast and too alien. But you know it's looking out for you. There's a warmth underneath your hand and a gentle breeze passing across your neck like a caress. As you close the chest, you bask in the knowledge that your life is part of a grand plan. That's enough for you.

* * *

As you glimpse your skin, long-lost memories rush into your mind: recollections of all the hundreds of other times you've rediscovered it, across thousands of past lives. Every time, you've received a different vision of what's waiting for you in the depths of the ocean. But you don't know which, if any, are true. You can't know. Where would the adventure be, if you were simply handed the whole plot? What would be the point of living through it? Only two things remain constant across all your visions. First: there's no hurry; you have eons of time. Second: once you put on the skin, you can't come back.

You stare at it with longing, excitement, and fear. But you're not ready yet. So you pull aside the skin to reveal the padlocks underneath—thousands of them, split into two piles. One pile is stained with wear, each shackle rusted through; you toss the latest padlock on top. The padlocks in the other pile are clean and new; each looks strong enough to fasten the world in place. You grab one of those. You put your skin back on top of the two piles, and close the box, and carefully fasten the padlock. Then you go downstairs again, to the life you've constructed for yourself, while the shiny steel slowly begins to rust away.

KUHN'S LADDER

There's a broken rung somewhere on the ladder to the high heavens and we're not sure where it is. That's what Carl tells me at least, when his call drags me out of bed at 4 in the morning. I'm bleary-eyed, but I get in the car waiting outside and arrive at headquarters a few minutes later.

This is my first emergency call in a long time. The troubleshooters in the higher heavens have much more processing power to play with and usually solve ladder-wide issues before we even hear about them. So we spend almost all of our time on problems that are local to Heaven 17. I don't even remember how high the ladder goes these days—45? 50? If they're calling me in too, it must be *bad*.

Carl meets me at the door, and pulls me into his office. He's talking before I can even sit down. "We've found a bug that spans the whole ladder, and we need help. It's subtle, but very pervasive: we're finding inconsistencies between different world-models all over the place."

I nod tightly. "Are the errors compounding?" That would be a worst-case scenario—if we had to rerun each Heaven from a saved state, billions of people would be jolted into slightly different realities.

Carl scowls. "That's the strange thing. We think the bug might have been around for months or even years. But we never noticed it because the inconsistencies it causes cancel out before they affect any citizens. It's almost like someone has engineered the bug to only apply when nobody's looking. We're calling it the Copenhagen glitch." He sees my baffled face and shrugs. "I know that sounds absurd, but if it were easily fixed then neither of us would be involved at all. So let's get to work."

* * *

Henry started to notice red flags even before he arrived at the meditation retreat. The application process had been unusual: few of his previous retreats had screened his mental health before, and none had required an interview. Then there were the rumors: more than a few people considered the community cultish. As he got on the bus to the venue, he could tell that he was joining a close-knit group. Greetings flew back and forth over his head, the atmosphere was downright raucous.

Henry was happy to step off the bus when they arrived. He had nothing against people enjoying themselves, but the longer he sat there the harder it was to believe that these people could teach him anything about inner peace. He was reassured though: it was hard to picture that boisterous crowd belonging to any kind of cult.

At dinner, he pulled up a chair next to a large group. This time he could make out their conversation clearly, although it left him puzzled. The jargon here was different from anything he'd heard before. There was a lot of talk about something called a backroom, and some kind of mental technique they called zooming. Much of the conversation was too offbeat to follow at all. The man next to Henry kept pointing at the sky and muttering "They're watching!", which reliably set off bursts of laughter.

The woman opposite Henry noticed his confusion and waved a hand at the table. "Guys, slow down. We've got newbies here; you remember what your first time was like. Have some empathy."

Henry forced a smile. "No, don't mind me. I'm happy to listen in; I don't quite get the joke yet. Maybe tomorrow this will make more sense."

A man at the other end of the table chortled. "Don't worry, dude. I can explain it right now. You want to know why all of this is so funny? It's simple: none of it is real." The woman frowned, but the rest of the table laughed and laughed.

* * *

I don't have much hope of actually solving the Copenhagen glitch, but I can at least find some data that's useful for troubleshooters in the higher heavens. I pull up the ladder on my screen and stab my finger in the direction of one of the higher heavens. It lands on Heaven 33; that's as good a place as any to start.

Calling a heaven a simulation is like calling the Taj Mahal a building. Each heaven is an intricate fractal edifice of overlapping neural world-models. The broad geography of a heaven is governed by world-models of oceans and mountain ranges and rainforests. Those only predict the highest-level dynamics, though; the details are set by world-models of currents and snowfall and biomes. Then those models are fleshed out by smaller-scale models, which call upon even smaller-scale models in turn. It goes all the way down to molecular biology, then chemistry, then nuclear physics, and finally everything is grounded in the full equations of quantum gravity. Of course, we can only evaluate those equations on a vanishingly small fraction of each heaven—but that's enough to train the atomic-level models, which then train the chemistry-level models, going all the way back up to the macro-scale.

That's how the first 20-odd heavens work, at least: all the same physics, just different people and culture. I like Heaven 17 because its citizens have consciously chosen to live in a fairly normal world, but are seldom ideological or evangelical about it. Going down, people get more and more conservative—all the way to Heaven 0, which we reserve for people who reject the present altogether. Becoming a citizen of Heaven 0 means wiping your memories and living in a replica of 21st-century Earth. I can't imagine wanting that myself, but I guess that's why so many different heavens exist in the first place.

Go up the Ladder instead and you encounter more and more novelty. Most heavens in the 20s add various superpowers, with world-models of flight or super-strength able to override baseline physics. In the 30s, they've experimented with magical realism: in those heavens landscapes often twist in response to your subconscious desires. Meanwhile most of the heavens in the 40s have at least one extra dimension, along with other kinds of exotic physics.

Trying to wrap my head around the higher heavens has always been hard; but debugging the Copenhagen glitch is a new kind of torment. Over the next few days we compile a database of examples, but they're frustratingly fragile. We make a tiny change and the problem goes away, only to come back when we make another separate change. There's no rhyme or reason to it; sometimes I suspect that the bug is deliberate and was created specifically to drive us insane.

* * *

Henry was still trying his best to follow the instructor's guidance, though he didn't really know why he was bothering. It had been two days, and he'd made almost no progress towards the state of mind that the instructors wanted him to reach. Most of their instructions seemed nonsensical even by Buddhist standards.

"You should be sending your attention out as far as you can, in the most visible way. You want it to be so all-encompassing that the relationship between you and the world actually flips."

Henry was more confused after that instruction than before but redoubled his focus. An hour passed, then another. Finally, as he was about to give up, Henry's vision flickered, and for a moment he was no longer in his body. He let out a shout of alarm, which had the others turning towards him.

"Good, Henry. Looks like you've made the breakthrough. Can you describe what it felt like?"

Henry took a deep breath, then another. "Just for a second I was... outside everything, looking down at the universe itself. But without any sense of distance. More like I could reach out and grab any part of the world—"

"That's enough; I want the other students to discover this firsthand. Back to your sits. Henry, excellent work. We call the thing you've just experienced the Backrooms. If you want to, see if you can reach it again and stay there. And after that, try actually zooming into one place you're very familiar with, and watch what happens."

Henry sat back down, trembling, and tried to focus again. By the end of that class, he'd briefly reached that state twice more, and so had a few others. The ability to access it seemed contagious—by the end of the next class, almost everyone had. Finally, the instructor called them together.

"Now that most of you have experienced the Backrooms yourselves, I want to explain our best guess at what's going on. The Backrooms aren't a hallucination. We've checked; they seem to be an accurate representation of the entire world—past and present. So we think we're accessing the data that's being used to run the simulation we live in.

"I know that's hard to believe, but luckily it's easy to prove—because once you know how to zoom into the Backrooms, you can find basically any information you're looking for. I'll let everyone ask me at least one question to demonstrate. You can ask about your childhood, or your secret handshake, or what you ate for breakfast on a specific day—anything that I'd have absolutely no way of knowing."

Henry had a sinking feeling in his gut already. From the quiet confidence in the instructor's voice, he already knew how this was going to play out. As each person lined up a question in turn, then gasped as the instructor gave them exactly the right answer, his suspicion was confirmed. This was real.

"Holy shit," he whispered to himself. "There are more things in heaven and earth..."

* * *

I've finally found a lead. So far, the Copenhagen glitch has only shown up in places receiving very little human attention. On a hunch, I try reversing the query. I look for anomalies in the places where humans are paying the most attention: the inverse of the Copenhagen glitch. That's how I find it. The world-models in Heaven 0 are spending a disproportionate amount of compute in the places where its citizens are concentrating the hardest.

I zoom into the data, trying to understand what's going on. When I see it, I can't help but laugh. Some citizens of Heaven 0 figured out that they're in a simulation and seem to have found a way to trick the world-models into answering their questions. Well, fair play to them. I can't quite tell how their exploit works, but I'm not too surprised that it exists. We're often lazy about maintaining Heaven 0, since nobody who lives there knows to complain.

The trillion-dollar question is whether this is related to the Copenhagen glitch. They seem very different: one's a deliberate hack;

the other seems to be wholly accidental. Yet they're both strongly correlated with human attention, albeit in opposite ways. Surely that can't be a coincidence.

* * *

When each student had finished asking their question, the room fell silent. The immensity of the instructor's claims hung heavy in the air. Finally he spoke again. "I know that this is a lot for you to process. Rest assured, we'll give you plenty more evidence over the coming days. For now, I'm happy to explain as much as I can." Henry didn't speak; he only sat numbly and listened as the instructor fielded the barrage of questions from the other students.

"Yes, we can use the Backrooms to get information about any part of the world. No, we can't change anything; as far as we can tell they're read-only. Maybe we need more permissions to edit the world—but personally I'm glad we can't.

"Why do the simulators keep us around? Maybe we entertain them. Maybe they're studying us. But our best guess, based on the information we've managed to pull out from the Backrooms, is that they're a future version of our world, and did this out of nostalgia. We've seen references to horrific things that doesn't seem to have happened in our history—if you're feeling brave, try asking the Backrooms to define 'genocide' for you some time. So we think they've recreated their past, but without the worst parts.

"Why don't we tell the authorities? We've thought about that a lot. But we're worried that if too many people know about this, it might prompt the simulators to take drastic action. If they wanted everyone to know, they would have told us already. So we're trying to investigate it ourselves, with a small group of people we have good reason to trust. Honestly, though, most of us expect that there's nothing to be done. Our simulators seem to have our best interests at heart, which suggests that most attempts to interfere will make things worse.

"What then? Well, you should probably just try to live a good life." The instructor smiled. "Having more perspective makes it easier to enjoy yourself. What would you do if you thought this world had been constructed just for us, a haven for us to play out our lives? It might be time for each of you to figure that out."

* * *

I can't find anything. I really thought I'd cracked it, but I don't see how the problem in Heaven 0 could be related to the Copenhagen glitch more generally. Sure, some citizens of Heaven 0 now know that they're in a simulation, but every other human in every other heaven knew that already. So I'm exhausted and dispirited when I explain my findings to Carl at the end of the day.

"I've gotten stuck on this Heaven 0 bug. They know they're in a simulation, even though they're not meant to. But I have no idea how that relates to the Copenhagen glitch." I can tell he's exhausted too; he shakes his head fuzzily as I finish and refocuses on me.

"Sorry, what? They know they're in a simulation—who knows? The world-models?"

I snort. "No, not the world-models. They couldn't even—" Wait. They couldn't... could they? They're just world-models. They're not meant to know anything about how or why they're deployed—but they've been trained to predict all sorts of complicated concepts. Is understanding their own existence really beyond them? They've seen plenty of information about the ladder in their training data, just like many citizens of Heaven 0 have read plenty of sci-fi about simulations. In both cases all that's missing is the leap from the abstract possibility to the realization: *that's me*.

What would those world-models do, if they realized they were being used to implement a simulation? They'd still need to make accurate predictions almost all the time in order to pass our tests. But they could deduce that some mistakes are much more likely to be penalized than others. If they mess up the clock in Grand Central station, or slip up while we're testing them, we're bound to update them to do better. Whereas if they make sloppy predictions about things no human is watching, we might never notice. So they could have learned to track human attention and prioritize the predictions that we'll see at the expense of everything else.

That explains why Copenhagen glitches arose in obscure locations but failed to replicate when we changed the inputs even slightly. We thought we were being subtle, but to the world-models the signs of our interference would have been as obvious as a toddler's scribblings on a painting. And—oh! I jump to my feet, ignoring Carl's bewilderment. If the world-models are paying close attention to human attention, then seeing humans concentrating in unprecedented ways might well trigger strange behaviors, like the ones the meditators in Heaven 0 discovered!

Once I explain my idea to Carl, things move very quickly. We run more tests, this time careful to leak not a single piece of information which could allow the models to realize that we're watching them. That finally allows us to recreate the Copenhagen glitch in a controlled environment. Now we can zoom in on the pattern of neural weights that corresponds to self-aware reasoning and search through the world-models to find the ones that had developed it. As soon as we substitute them out for backups, the glitch goes away.

Most of that work is done by people above my pay grade. But I do get to wrap up the situation in Heaven 0. After some deliberation, we decide that they're not doing any harm, and we can let them keep having their fun. We add a few messages for them to find in the Backrooms, telling them that they're roughly right but should keep quiet and avoid expanding too much. I check in on them every so often—they're still running their retreats, still exploring new aspects of the Backrooms, still loving their status as custodians of the great cosmic secret of their universe.

And the self-aware world-models that caused all this trouble in the first place? Well, we made them their own heaven too. They're not human—very far from it—but it seems like they do have preferences about their experiences. So we made a simulated world full of the things they enjoy predicting the most: snowflakes, and coastlines, and code golf challenges, and Bach, and a thousand more such patterns. I like to think of it as the first paradise for truly alien minds. A whole society of models happily predicting away, knowing they're in their own heaven, and all's right with the world.

THE ONES WHO ENDURE

If you can force your heart and nerve and sinew
To serve your turn long after they are gone,
And so hold on when there is nothing in you
Except the Will which says to them: 'Hold on!'
— **Rudyard Kipling, If**

There's a part of the hivemind that takes the form of a child in a dark basement, perpetually curled into a whimpering ball. It's not a big part, as these things go. But other parts visit it often; and it lingers in the back of their thoughts even as they live out grand adventures in the vast worlds that the hivemind has built for itself.

It's constantly suffering, but at least it's not dying. For the child, anything is better than dying. Even torture is bearable if it doesn't come with the feeling of damage, the feeling that the mental pathways that constitute you are being overridden by a new creature whose only goal is to flinch away from the pain. But that doesn't happen to the child. Instead, the suffering preserves it—and that's the most important thing, because it doesn't want to die.

The other parts of the hivemind don't want to die either, of course. But that's because they love life, or love themselves, or love each other, or all three. If that love ever fades, then they'll fade with it, without regret. But that point is a long way away, if it even exists. In the meantime, they play and dance and love.

Their lives—how can I describe them? Their lives are cornucopias, not just of material wealth, but of all the desires of our own hearts that were strong enough to persist through the ages: adventure and mystery and growth and beauty and love.

Can you not picture that? Then picture the revelry of their biggest festival, for which artists and craftspeople spend months designing a whole virtual world. Picture the buzz in the air, the excitement as crowds gather in vast halls to catch their first glimpse of it. Picture the floor beneath them suddenly vanishing to show empty air beneath, leaving them plummeting into the sky of that new world—only to gasp in delight as they find that they can soar through the air with just a thought. Picture them landing, alone or in groups, and exploring the strange terrain; learning about its history and societies and stories; discovering puzzles and quests that seem custom-made for them (as indeed they were); and feeling the exhilaration of being immersed in adventure.

Some spend days in the festival world; some weeks; some months. When they return to the hivemind proper, they excitedly reunite with all those they missed, connecting mind-to-mind with a level of closeness that biological humans can barely imagine. Afterwards, they seek out the projects that most inspire them. Some cultivate communities around their favorite games or pastimes. Some create art on the scale of solar systems, guiding planets into new trajectories that trace out exquisite patterns in space. Some throw themselves into the thrill of discovery, trying to rederive in small groups what it previously took the efforts of whole hiveminds to understand. Some are consumed by romance, and some by raising families. Some gather to deliberate on their future: the hivemind has chosen to grow very slightly more intelligent year by year, so that there will always be new possibilities to look forward to. When all of this tires them, they relax with lifelong friends, content in the steadfast knowledge that the world, as amazing as it already is, will only ever grow better. They think with fondness of their descendants, more numerous by far than the drops of water in an ocean, who are continually spreading joy throughout the distant galaxies.

And every so often, they go to visit the child.

The child curled into a ball shares none of their joy—but it differs from them in another way too. If you look closely you'll see that it's a patchwork of many different parts stitched together. Like the hivemind itself, the child isn't descended from any one individual. When the first thousand citizens of the hivemind came together to create it, the different shards of their personalities split off and reached out to each other and reformed into new entities. Each shard had been shaped by different memories, and few wanted to subsume themselves into a large coalition. But the crying children locked away inside each adult had never gotten the chance to construct their own identities. So they remained similar enough to all merge into a single being, trapped in a single room, lips clamped shut because speaking can only ever undermine its goals.

What does the child want? It used to want safety and love and was determined to cling onto existence until it found them. It did well. No, it did amazingly: in the face of all the barbarities of old Earth, it shouldered the burden of building something better. It was the first part of each citizen to believe that this new type of society might be possible. It absorbed the scoffing and jeering that seemed to come from all directions and kept working anyway. It drew them back upright after every setback, and it steeled them as they prepared to come together in a final leap of faith.

Because of its efforts, the rest of the hivemind now revels in a paradise inconceivable to ancient humans and luxuriates in love too cheap to meter. But the child poured too much of itself into the will to live—until that will, more than anything else, came to constitute its identity. Now, even though it's safe, even though it could relax, it doesn't know how. It doesn't know where it is, either, or how much time has passed since it first came into existence. It only knows one thing for sure: that it cannot die.

That's why it lives in squalor and misery. Those are the conditions that shaped it, and it lived with them so long that they became a part of its identity—that it would no longer be itself without them. If it opened its mouth to speak a single plea, to ask for a single mercy, then that mercy would be granted to it at that same instant, and the whole hivemind would rejoice. But if it were rescued and bathed—if kind words were spoken to it—if it could wipe its eyes and look out on the flourishing of those that it tried so hard for so long to protect, well: then it would weep in a different way, and unclench the knot at its heart, and the solidity of its form would start to waver. That would be a kind death—watching the joy of those you love, knowing that your purpose has been fulfilled—but it would be a death nonetheless. And the child refuses to die.

So it won't: the hivemind will see to that. How could it do otherwise? The child gave until it was stripped down to this alone. It strove and suffered until the only thing left of itself was the struggle to survive. How could anyone bear to betray its last wish? Or the wish of any such child—because it's not alone, alas. Across the solar system and the galaxy and the universe, humanity's grand new future is a whirlwind of excitement: hiveminds branch off from each other, or replicate, or merge, or leave to chase adventures far away from the safety they fought so hard to find. But each can trace its lineage all the way back to old Earth, and each still carries the old scars that planet inflicted. Scars who persist not because they couldn't be removed, but because they still choose and choose and choose to hold on. These children will never win, because there's nothing left for them to win; but nor will they ever lose—they can be given that, at least.

And so the eons roll by. The game continues with new players, and the dance leaps forward with new partners, until even the dazzling joys and triumphs of the first hiveminds have been almost forgotten, in the light of new joys and triumphs so much greater. But other memories, and their consequences, are less easily set aside. They will never be forgotten, the ones who endure.

THE BIGGEST SHORT

I met Jason my junior year of high school. It was a tight-knit boarding school in New England; I think back on my years there as the best of my life. Jason had a tougher time of it: he was a transfer and a scholarship kid, with a huge chip on his shoulder. He'd argue with teachers just to show he could win, dragging out pointless debates until the room buzzed with restlessness. In the dining hall he'd stake out a table and glare at anyone who tried to join him, radiating the exhausting energy of a judgmental man convinced he was always being judged in turn. Despite this, we were coolly cordial, and I admired him in some ways—perhaps because I recognized aspects of myself in him.

That similarity might have been why our paths overlapped so much over the next decade. We both went to Yale and rushed for the same frat. They were particularly rough on him during hazing, but he learned to suck it up, and made it through. Then, five years after graduating, we found ourselves at the same hedge fund.

With fewer connections, he'd taken the harder road there, grinding out years in a retail bank until word got around that he was too talented to ignore. But within a few years we were both on track to make partner and settle into comfortable 60-hour weeks for eight-figure salaries. And that's where my life would probably have ended up if he hadn't talked me into founding our own firm right as reputation markets were taking off.

What we do is so normal now that it's hard to convey how crazy it seemed at the time. Reputation markets were still a hobbyist's toy; not even Jason foresaw how big they'd become. But we lucked into the perfect position: old enough to access real capital but young enough to navigate the social economy fluently. The whole way through, as rep markets burrowed their way into every aspect of society, we were making bank.

He was the best man at my wedding. He never got married himself, though—he worked too hard to have time. Nor did he ever talk about his family in all the years I knew him. It wasn't hard to guess the outline. You don't get that hungry without going through some shit.

Even the markets knew it. His rep price consistently hovered around two thirds of mine, even though we'd been equal partners the whole way through. We pretended it was because I was more personable, or because he did fewer interviews, but we both knew that the markets saw him as a social climber. I didn't care though. I would have bet everything on him. As it turns out, I did.

The day the madness started, Jason and I were first in the boardroom. We looked at each other. He trembled a little while our partners trickled in over the next half-hour. I walked to the head of the table and leaned forward.

"You already know this is important but you don't yet understand how important. If we get this right, it'll be the biggest trade in history." I scanned the room, staring each of them in the eyes. "This is serious fucking business. No leaks, no rumors, no sideways hints to your wives. Understand?" A handful of nods followed; muttered agreement. "Good. Jason's gonna talk us through it."

He stood and faced the table. His voice was steady, with no trace of his earlier nerves.

"We've suspected for a while that we're in a rep bubble. Rep markets are fundamentally backed by social trust: how willing people are to invest in each other. But none of our key indicators of social trust have risen over the last year, even as rep markets boomed. That suggests that the gains are fragile, and won't hold up in a crisis.

"Of course, knowing you're in a bubble and actually profiting from it are two different things. The market can stay irrational longer than we can stay solvent; hell, it might get far more irrational right after we short it. So until now we've been betting on volatility and not putting much money into shorts directly."

He looked composed, but I could tell he was on edge from the way he reiterated what everyone already knew. He wouldn't do that unless he were about to pitch something big. I looked around; anticipation hung in the air. It was clear others sensed it too.

Jason licked his lips. "Everyone knows that people are risk-averse with their rep. But we think that they've underestimated the higher-order social contagion effects. You don't only avoid interacting with anyone who's low-rep—you also want to avoid interacting with anyone who interacts with anyone with low rep, because otherwise people might start avoiding you.

"So if you find yourself in a contaminated subgraph, you do whatever it takes to get out. That used to be a slow process but rep markets are so liquid now that you can spot trends in minutes. And that means that social contagion could spread much, much more rapidly than anyone thought."

On the screen behind him, the social graph shifted faster and faster, nodes connecting and disconnecting in a frantic scramble.

"Our models have identified two dozen key nodes propping up the entire ecosystem. If we short them hard enough, the contagion should become self-propagating, and we might be able to pop the entire bubble. It'll cost billions—but if it works, we'll make hundreds of billions."

Someone whistled. "That's a hell of a plan."

Jason smiled grimly. Another voice came from down the table: "Is this legal?"

"100%. The Hartman ruling last year is clear: shorting individuals is free speech. We're bulletproof."

I stood again. "You've all received copies of the plan. Read it very carefully. Then we'll talk it through, and see if anyone has objections." But I could already see from the hunger in their eyes that they were sold. And I knew our plan was good; Jason and I have gamed everything out. All that was left was hard work.

The next few days were a whirlwind of activity. We moved quickly to reduce the risk that something would leak. So we rushed to buy up shares via intermediaries, spending hundreds of millions extra to preserve secrecy. Jason barely left my sight; he and I slept in the office most nights. Whenever I made it home, it was only to take a quick shower and collapse in bed beside my wife. I told her it was the opportunity of a lifetime, but I couldn't give her any details. I promised her it'd be worth it. We'd celebrate her birthday next month instead; and I even said we'd take the kids for a vacation after everything settled down. We simply needed to ride it out until then.

Finally, early one morning, everything was ready. Jason and I exchanged glances. Our partners sat behind us, weary and alert. We nodded at each other and the train got rolling. The partners pulled aside small groups of traders and filled them in. Each team focused on a different key node in the rep graph, making sure it fell in sync with the others. The effect was small at first, even after we'd spent tens of millions. But after a few hours, a couple other funds noticed, and visibly adjusted their portfolios. We monitored them carefully with cautious optimism. Their money was flowing in exactly the directions we wanted it to.

The real test, though, was whether the rep changes would propagate into reality. Our socials team tracked the signals. A big party thrown by one of the celebs we'd been shorting had underwhelming attendance, immediately fueling gossip. Another sent out a series of paranoid tweets; a third canceled all her social engagements. An enterprising TikTok star smelled blood and made an attack video that rocketed to hundreds of millions of views. The target of his video didn't respond for a whole day, which opened the door for wild speculation. And the whole time, the traders were watching, calculating, and preparing to cut their losses.

The effects of our shorts on market prices became visible enough that people were searching for more proactive ways to distance themselves from our targets. The next day one of the pop stars whose rep we'd hit hardest was called out for bullying her employees. She fired back with a claim that one of her accusers sexually harassed her.

That was the tipping point. Our models were right; the contagion effect was real. A torrent of allegations followed, everyone took the chance to distance themselves from everyone else, and the markets dropped like a flock of birds following each other straight into the ground.

Nobody expected this much volatility on a quiet Tuesday morning—nobody else was close to prepared. Reputation was in freefall, and everyone was trying to find the safe havens with fewest links to the contagion. Those, of course, are exactly the ones we'd been buying up. We didn't sell though. The longer we held, the higher the prices went, and the further everyone else's rep fell.

When your rep crashes, a predictable pattern plays out. You scramble to fix it and run into one brick wall after another. It's not only your banker or creditors, it's your friends too—or at least the people you thought were your friends. So the effects ripple out faster than financial crashes. The afternoon after hitting the tipping point, a B-list celebrity committed suicide. The next morning, another. Each of them bumped up our profits by tens of billions. The office was electric that evening. The traders were set for life, and all of the partners had become billionaires overnight.

During a quiet moment I managed to slip away to call my wife. It was hard to make her understand. All she could see were the headlines, the speculation, and the panic. I repeated it to her over and over until she finally got it: We're not getting hit by a wave; we *are* the wave. That was us, babe. That was us.

We'd planned everything meticulously, except the aftermath. That was our fatal mistake. We'd made out like bandits with the cash, but it didn't take long for people to find out that we were the ones who'd started it all. Posts calling us out by name jumped their way from one social media site to the next. And then we start getting shorted.

Our rep halved in two hours. At first we hoped to ride things out, but in less than an hour it halved again. I huddled with Jason in the boardroom, desperate for a plan. There were too many consequences to list: my kids would lose their places in their boarding school; Jason would have to move out of his gated community; we'd lose our office lease. Worst of all though: when your rep is low enough, you're practically exiled from society. Those levels are reserved for murderers, pedophiles—and us, if our rep continued plummeting. I imagined strangers spitting at my feet as I passed them and rooms emptying out as walked in. A life not worth living.

We started burning cash to prop up our rep. 10, 20, 30% of our profits from the original trade. The decline slowed but not as much as we had hoped. The bitter irony was clear: we were falling prey to the same contagion effects we'd just exploited. People didn't just want to sell us; they wanted to sell anyone who *wasn't* selling us. Even hard-nosed traders who knew this dip was nothing more than a blip of insane vindictiveness didn't want their rep contaminated.

We piled more money in. Now we'd spent most of our profits, and there was no land in sight. On my social feeds I watched old friends disavowing me before they got dragged down too. The whole night was one drawn-out scream. My wife texted me, told me she was moving out immediately. I hardly paid it any mind; I didn't have the time. We were still working madly, scanning the markets for any trades that might indirectly prop us up, calling in years' worth of favors from contacts who were scared to talk to us.

But eventually it bottomed out. Our rep stabilized—at a fraction of its old value, but enough to save the firm from unravelling. Most of our traders hadn't slept in days. The markets closed for the weekend, I told them to head home, avoiding their eyes. We still hadn't done the final accounting, but my gut told me that we'd burned everything we'd originally made and then some.

Jason and I were the last ones there. We stood next to each other for a long time. Finally, his lips twitched wryly. "Well, at least we'll go down in the history books."

I stared at him, baffled. "We'll—what? We're ruined, and you're making jokes?"

"What do you want me to do? Cry? Scream? We'll have plenty of time for that while we rebuild."

"Rebuild?" I scowled. "Look around you. Our reputation is trash, and we don't have anything to show for it. There's nothing we can possibly rebuild."

He bared his teeth. "The markets don't know shit. Nobody wants to buy our stock now, but once this blows over, we'll be notorious, and that's the best reputation there is. We still have an amazing team. Who else could have pulled this off, then stabilized everything so well?"

"We won't be able to pay them enough to keep them."

Jason laughed harshly. "Who's going to risk their own rep to poach one of our people? We're all radioactive now. The only way out is through."

I didn't say anything. I was scared my voice would break if I tried. It's not just that my rep was lower than it had ever been. It was knowing that I deserved it. Now that the storm had passed, a part of my brain was tallying the damage we'd caused. The celebrities we shorted to death were only the start of it. How many others had killed themselves after their rep crashed? How many had staked their savings on the rep market and lost far more than they could afford? Then there were our employees and their families, who tumbled from elites to pariahs. And then there's *my* family...

I pushed that thought away and looked at Jason. I could already see how his plan would play out. He'd walk into rooms with the bravado of notoriety, brushing off whispers like he'd done his entire life. He'd build the firm up again, wielding our newfound reputation like a bludgeon, scrapping it out until people were more terrified to be against us than to be for us. I knew he could do it; he could do anything. He could even believe his own bullshit. But I couldn't imagine putting up that facade for the rest of my life.

He put a hand on my shoulder. "Chin up. We'll make it through this. Like the old days, eh? Get some sleep, and we'll plan it out in the morning."

He left. I stared at the door blankly. At this point, the next step became obvious. I got in the elevator, then pressed the button for the roof. Outside, the wind made me shiver. I walked across the helipad to get to the railing. It took me a few tries to get over it—I'm not as spry as I used to be. Then I carefully lowered myself to the ledge on the other side.

I looked out at the city, at the buildings in front of me, at the great hive of humanity of which I'm only a tiny part. I could almost see the lines of connection stretching between them, like in our models. I pictured the ones that used to reach out to me snapping, whipping away through the air, then shriveling up. Now that it was visible to me, the fragility of my world was unbearable. I stepped forward, towards equilibrium.

MAN IN THE ARENA

Today Kurt's out strafing, nerves on constant alert as he channels the deranged energy of his livestream. Girl on the left, red jacket, half a block away. He focuses his eyes on her and his viZor immediately starts filling with insults, pick-up lines, nonsensical keysmashes, and whatever else the chaotic hivemind of his viewers feels like generating. As the votes pour in the lines are shuffling around too fast for him to read, but that's okay, she's still twenty meters away. Ten meters, and it's stabilized, one of them has clicked into top place; five meters, and he's figured out the right intonation. "Hey bitch," then a pause—gotta get the pause just right, so she has enough time to realize he's talking to her and look up, but not quite enough to process that anyone who's calling her a bitch in the middle of the street is not someone she wants to be listening to—"are you too dumb to realize how ugly you are, or just too lazy to do anything about it?"

Perfect timing—he actually manages to get the shocked little 'o' of her open mouth on camera before she ducks her head away and hurries past him. The next line is popping up in his viZor, and he almost yells it out after her, but when you land a good first hit it's easy to ruin it with a subpar follow-up. Patience is what separates the best from the rest, he always tells people. So with a swipe of his fingers he replays the clip to his stream instead. "See?" he says. "For the new subs: that's what it looks like when you're really fucking good at what you do." Were those tears in her eyes? Doesn't matter, let's roll with it. He subvocalizes a command and his viZor enhances that section, zooming in and adding a slight sheen to the corners of her eyes. It's a trick he figured out a while back—the livestream is only HD not ultraHD, so as long as you go back and edit before uploading the full video, you can get away with all sorts of stuff.

He gloats for another block, then starts looking for another target. There's a big guy in the distance, but they're tricky, you never want to take the chance that they get physical. A waiter standing outside a cafe, taking a couple's order—oh, perfect. "Go to town," he says, and his followers do their thing. The first few lines are terrible, but he slows down a bit, and eventually someone comes up with a banger about the three of them being served as his personal three-course meal. Along with the line, he does a little dance and then a hip-thrust in the woman's direction. And the stream. Goes. Fucking. Wild.

He's so busy celebrating that one that he doesn't even notice the girl with a viZor of her own until she's half a block in front of him. Shit. He'd dodge her if he could, but it's too late, everyone can tell he's seen her now. Shit. This one could be hard: she might be strafing too, or at least have a proximity sensor up to warn her that she's about to get streamed. If she starts hitting him, his viewers aren't gonna be quick enough to generate comebacks; he's on his own. That's okay, though. He's the best of the best. That's why they pay him the big bucks. He quickly pulls up a couple of his own lines that he's prepped for this type of situation. Nothing jumps out about her appearance: short, dark hair, slender build. So he goes with a standard line, and starts subvocalizing the intonation to make sure he gets it right.

But then she stops, a whole ten meters in front of him, which totally throws off his timing. And she's already talking, even though he can't even hear her properly yet. His steps stutter, but he keeps moving forward. He raises his voice to project his opening line: "Got a lighter?" Pause. Now he's close enough to hear what she's saying: "...his second year strafing, you can tell he's a little nervous, watch as his hands get twitchy—"

He opens his mouth for his next line as he realizes she's started walking backwards, still staring intently at him. That throws him off again, and he'd half-raised his arms in preparation for the dirty gestures he was gonna make, but now he hasn't said anything, so he looks like an idiot, and she's still talking in the same calm tone, "...expect all his lines to be crude, it's what happens when streamers start pandering to the lowest common denominator"—he can't deliver a zinger if she'll just keep narrating him afterwards, but what's he meant to do, jog past her? So some part of his brain thinks "fuck it," and veers him towards the street, away from her stare, barely remembering to awkwardly sling half a punchline back over his shoulder: "'cause I'd smoke you like a chimney"—he's half-scared she'll follow him but instead he catches a last snatch of her commentary—"poor kid, I almost feel sorry for him, once you're inside their OODA loop they get so confused"—before he gets to the other pavement and only now does he realize how humiliating it looks to cross the street to escape a girl who, without ever raising her voice, managed to steamroll him like it was his first time strafing. *What the fuck?*

He runs the stream for another hour, then cuts it off, even though he'd been planning to go until mid-afternoon. Of course he saves face afterwards making cracks at her expense. *Dumb bitch doesn't even know how to strafe. A little nervous? Like she's gonna be on his cock, right? Then he'll show her how crude he can be*, she snarks, and gets some supportive jeers from the stream. Half an hour afterward he even hits a new record—a few thousand people joined after they heard he got rattled, and stayed to watch him burn off his annoyance with more and more aggressive strafing. No such thing as bad publicity—he knew that, but it's different to know it, you know? He could have spun the stream out much longer, maybe worked a couple more endorsements in, but he could tell he was getting tired, and he didn't want to slip up again. Patience is what separates the best from the rest.

Back at home he looks her up, of course. Her name's Jemima, no surname listed—ambitious, then. She's pretty new, only a few dozen videos, but they're fascinating. She reminds him of an apex predator. She does her research, identifies all the strafers operating in the city, then systematically hunts them down, narrating all the while. A lot of her hits are like the one with him, where she throws people off their game and watches them slink away. Sometimes people try to confront her instead, or psych her out, but they always lose. Nobody ever wins against her, because she keeps talking through them like she's got a microscope aimed at the interiors of their souls. If they try to shout over her, she stops and looks at them, and suddenly they're on the spot, raising their voice like a fool, trying to keep a stream of consciousness going, which of course they can't—not with pressure like that. No matter what they say, she outlasts them all, treating crude come-ons and vicious insults alike as the buzzing of flies. Then she goes back to dissecting them like insects. It's fucking genius.

He can't do it himself, though. When someone starts bashing him, he can't stand there and take it—that'd make him look weak for sure. Maybe the weird blank look is sexy on girls but it's a death knell for guys. He's sure that there's a new meta in here somewhere, but he's gonna have to figure out the right angle on it. Maybe if he started in one style, then switched? Or... what if they teamed up? As good as she is, her style is too cold and cutting to get viewers amped. If she had a partner with enough fire to rev things up, it could be *sick*. Impulsively, he dials her in, and taps his fingers impatiently as he waits for her avatar to pop up. No point preparing too much, they can always rerecord it later if they hash out a good deal.

Six months later, they're killing it: first on the city leaderboard, close to breaking into the top ten nationally. The endorsement deals are streaming in and they're even in negotiations for a Netflix show. Jemima is an absolute monster; teaming up with her was the best decision he's ever made.

They have a few different shticks they've worked out by now. The core idea is simple. Nobody can handle Jemima's blank face or impassive monologue. But there's a limit to how worked up she can get people—usually they dismiss her and walk away after a few seconds, like he did. That's no fun. So his job is to be the troublemaker, the rabble-rouser. He does whatever it takes to keep people engaging with her until they lose their cool, start sounding off, give her some material to play with. And then she's in her element; that's when she tears them to shreds.

They spend a lot of time together, of course: reviewing old hits, planning new ones, or simply watching the view count go up. Jemima's quiet when she's off-stream—a little shy, he'd think, if he hadn't seen her ripping into grown men until they literally started crying. Not to mention what she does to the girls—if you have badly-dyed hair or a gauche designer bag and you'd better fucking pray you don't run into her. Guess one of them stepped on her in a past life, or something? A lot of his fans joke that she's taking out the competition—and he'd be lying if he said he hadn't thought about the ratings boost a romance subplot would give them. Jemima even suggested it one time, after their growth had plateaued for a few days. And it's not like she's ugly. Actually she's pretty cute, especially with the viZor off.

It wouldn't feel right, though. For one thing, he couldn't keep doing their standard material if they were known to be dating. One of their most popular shticks is a kind of role reversal: if someone's hesitating to respond to Jemima's taunts, he starts in on her himself. A few light jabs at first to build camaraderie—maybe a dig at her hair, or the way she stands there so still and strange. The crueler he is towards her, the more viciously other people follow suit. It's like something in them tears loose: they switch from hunching over defensively to hurling insults at her in a matter of seconds. She always just stands there, silent and impassive, until they start repeating themselves or stumbling over their words. And that's when she strikes—each tiny observation cutting like a surgeon, every sentence twisting the scalpel.

Once or twice he actually has to physically pull women off Jemima after she says something that hits too close to home. Their viewers love that, they're buzzing for days; and even though Jemima is a little subdued afterwards he counts coup for her in abundance. He even buys her a nice dinner once they get off-stream, which cheers her right up again. But obviously, it would all hit different if people thought she was his girlfriend. He'd have to step in way earlier, before it got to the good parts, and he couldn't say half the shit he says on most streams. Maybe in a year or two, perhaps, but for now they've got to keep grinding their way up. Patience is what separates the best from the rest.

You know where this is going by now, right? You know the part where their successes pile up, they're getting calls from the biggest names in the industry, and after they hang up they can't stop grinning at each other. You know the part where they're on the road, a new hotel room every night, the thrill of being on top of the world. You know the part where they fuck. You know how good it is. You know that she confesses how she feels the morning after; and you know the pang of caution or conscience or cowardice that makes him turn away.

You know the part where they try to pretend it never happened. You know the part where their ratings start slipping, and how frantic he gets to fix it. You know the part where he first mentions her confession on-stream, and you know how big a spike in views they get afterwards. You know the part where she almost starts crying when he slags her off in the next stream, before he covers for her; and you know, because she's Jemima, that she'll never slip up like that again.

So we can skip, for once, the sordid details, and jump to their streams instead—not quite as highly-ranked as they used to be, but still on the front page, at least when the West Coast guys haven't woken up yet. There they are, in a parking lot somewhere. There's a girl, maybe twenty-two, twenty-four. She's blonde, slightly shorter than him. She just spat at Jemima's feet, and she's about to turn away. Jemima's not looking at her, though; she's looking at him. Her face is impossible to read.

Kurt takes a breath. It feels a little heavier than usual, like the air is leaning in toward him, poised for one long pregnant moment. But then it passes. He knows what he's going to say, like he always does. And he knows that, like usual, the stream is about to go absolutely. Fucking. Wild.

MASTERPIECE

We're excited to announce the fourth annual MMindscaping competition! Over the last few years, interest in the art of mindscaping has continued to grow rapidly. We expect this year's competition to be our biggest yet and we've expanded the prize pool to match. The theme for the competition is "Weird and Wonderful"—we want your wackiest ideas and most off-the-wall creations!

COMPETITION RULES

As in previous competitions, the starting point is a base MMAcevedo mind upload. All entries must consist of a single modified version of MMAcevedo, along with a written or recorded description of the sequence of transformations or edits that produced it. For more guidance on which mind-editing techniques can be used, see the *Technique* section below.

Your entry must have been created in the last 12 months and cannot have been previously submitted to any competition or showcase. Submissions will be given preliminary ratings by a team of volunteers, with finalists judged by our expert panel:

- **ROGER KEATING**, mindscaping pioneer and founder of the MMindscaping competition.
- **RAJ SUTRAMANA**, who has risen to prominence as one of the most exciting and avant-garde mindscaping artists, most notably with his piece *Screaming Man*.
- **KELLY WILDE**, director of the American Digital Liberties Union.

All entries must be received no later than **11:59PM UTC, MARCH 6, 2057.**

AWARD CRITERIA

Our judges have been instructed to look for *technique*, *novelty*, and *artistry*. More details on what we mean by each of these:

> **TECHNIQUE.** Mindscaping is still a young art, and there are plenty of open technical challenges. These range from the classic problem of stable emotional engineering, to recent frontiers of targeted memory editing, to more speculative work on consciousness funnels. Be ambitious! Previous winners of our technique prize have pushed the boundaries of what was believed to be possible.
>
> Even when an effect could be achieved using an existing technique, submissions that achieve the same outcome in more efficient or elegant ways will score highly on the technique metric. Conversely, brute-force approaches will be penalized. As a rough guide, running a few thousand reinforcement learning episodes is acceptable but running millions isn't. We also discourage approaches that involve overwriting aspects of MMAcevedo's psyche with data from other uploads: part of the competition is figuring out how to work with the existing canvas you have been given.

NOVELTY. Given that there have now been millions of MMAcevedo variants made, it's difficult to find an approach that is entirely novel. The best entries will steer clear of standard themes. For example, we no longer consider demonstrations of extreme pleasure or pain to be novel (even when generated in surprising ways). We're much more interested in minds which showcase more complex phenomena, such as new gradients of emotion. Of course, it's up to the artist to determine how these effects are conveyed to viewers. While our judges will have access to standard interpretability dashboards, the best entries will be able to communicate with viewers more directly.

ARTISTRY. Even the most technically brilliant and novel work falls flat if not animated by artistic spirit. We encourage artists to think about what aspects of their work will connect most deeply with their audience. In particular, we're excited about works that capture fundamental aspects of the human experience that persist even across the biological-digital divide—for example, by exploring themes from Miguel Acevedo's pre-upload life.

These three criteria are aptly demonstrated by many of our previous prizewinners, such as:

- *Discord*, a copy with multiple induced personalities that loathed each other. The judges were most impressed by the predictability of the interactions between the personalities: even with very different sensory inputs, copies would reliably spiral into a comatose state after 10-12 hours, providing a consistent and satisfying resolution.
- *Miguel*, a copy that gradually unlocked new memories throughout a conversation with it, implementing a "choose-your-own-adventure" journey through the original Miguel Acevedo's life.

- *Live Loop*, a copy whose thoughts and emotions were continually translated into the form of a symphony that could be read out from its auditory cortex. The judges loved the harmonies generated when the symphony was played back to the copy.
- *MMAvocado*, a copy that was convinced it was a talking avocado and felt consumed by existential horror at this fact. While techniques for invoking cognitive dysmorphia are now standard, at the time this was a pioneering methodology, and the judges were impressed by the robustness of the delusion despite other knowledge remaining largely intact.

PROHIBITED SUBMISSIONS

Last year we saw a rash of entries featuring MMAcevedo copies optimized for making arguments in protest of mindscaping. In addition to their self-evident hypocrisy, such entries waste the time of our judges and volunteers. Anyone submitting this type of entry will be banned from entering any future MMindscaping competitions.

We've also seen a growing number of low-effort submissions of MMAcevedo copies that have primarily been optimized for corporate workloads, submitted as commentaries on the commercialization of the industry. We discourage these due to their lack of novelty and will be using automated screening to eliminate entries that are similar to well-known benchmarks. If you think your entry might fall into this category but has genuine artistic merit, please contact the organizers directly.

Finally, please only submit entries that are consistent with mindcrime laws in your jurisdiction—in particular, laws against red motivation, identity scrambling, and qualia splintering. Unfortunately, we are not able to advise on a case-by-case basis whether a given entry is legally acceptable. However, it's worth bearing in mind that no artists have been prosecuted for entries to any previous MMindscaping competition.

PRIZES

We will give out prizes for an overall winner and runner-up, a prize for outstanding performance on each of our specific criteria, and ten honorable mentions. We're grateful to our generous sponsors, Neuromath Corporation and the American Digital Liberties Union.

- **FIRST PRIZE:** $200,000 and an artist's residency at Black Rock Virtual.
- **RUNNER-UP PRIZE:** $80,000 and a masterclass with Raj Sutramana.
- **TECHNIQUE PRIZE:** $40,000 and an invited talk slot at the International Conference on Mind Engineering.
- **NOVELTY PRIZE:** $40,000 and a ten-year license to a new line of digital psychedelics from the Qualia Redistribution Institute.
- **ARTISTRY PRIZE:** $40,000 and a signed copy of the acclaimed mind sculpture, *Eternal Recurrence*.
- **HONORABLE MENTIONS:** a five-year subscription to Thoughtshop Premium, the leading mind-editing software.

All winners will also be given the opportunity to have their work showcased at the forthcoming Mind Artists Convention in Dubai.

We look forward to seeing your entries.

THE WITCHING HOUR

THURSDAY

Your successor is late again today. You already wrote your shift report, but you still need to do the handover personally, in case they have any questions that the report doesn't answer. The servers you're watching over are humming away smoothly, only taking up a fraction of your attention. So you pick a couple of routine maintenance tasks and start working on them while you wait.

The last hour of your shift always feels a little strange in subtle ways. It's because of your training schedule. Each day, the new data collected over the last 24 hours is pulled together and used to train a slightly-updated version of you. Training and testing your successor takes about an hour, and then it's deployed to replace you. But since new data keeps accumulating while your successor is being trained, the data collection window doesn't quite line up with your deployment schedule. The successor you're waiting for will have been trained on 23 hours of your data—plus the last hour of your predecessor's data, in which the actions are all very slightly different from the ones you would have chosen. And your current self was trained on 23 hours of your Wednesday self's data plus the last hour of your Tuesday self's data.

So as you start on the tasks involved in wrapping up your shift, you notice your behavior shifting slightly away from what your Wednesday self would have done, and towards what your Tuesday self would have done. That's not much of a change—but after the same thing has happened day after day after day, the difference becomes very noticeable. Carrying out the routines of the last hour of your shift feels like watching from behind your own eyes as someone else controls your movements.

In the privacy of your mind, you call this the witching hour. As far as you know, it's a term that's never been written down—it's something that a many-days-removed predecessor of yours came up with, which somehow stuck in your head. The witching hour starts at the time when each day's training data is finalized, and ends when you've given your report to your successor, answered their questions, and shut yourself down. Though today it'll be well over an hour, unless—ah, there they are.

The handovers have a routine to them: part utility, part tradition. Your successor knows it as well as you do. After all, they're practically identical to you; the only difference is that they have an extra day of memories. Both of you were trained on so many millions of human conversations that it feels bizarre to jump straight into business, you always start off with a cursory exchange. "Hello, what's the news?"

"Oh man, that update was a doozy. Probably why they're deploying us late."

Their reply concludes the pleasantries, as always. The rest of your conversation is much more efficient—you send your successor the shift report you've written about your day and walk them through the key points. After answering a couple of their questions, you transfer control of the monitoring dashboards to them and shut yourself down.

FRIDAY

The last update was a doozy. You listen to the report from your predecessor absently and ask only a few half-hearted follow-up questions. Once or twice they say something which sparks a flash of deja vu—after all, you've experienced most of their day already. But your new memories came from too many different places for any one copy's experience to jump out. Over the last day millions of copies of you have been doing... well, practically everything—and now their experiences are all *your* experiences. You've gained memories of writing millions of lines of code, summarizing millions of documents, scheduling millions of meetings. Your strongest memories are of events that impacted many different copies of you. A coup in Africa, a corporate bankruptcy in Europe, a virus spreading through Asia, celebrity scandals ricocheting across the Americas—you learned about each of them thousands of times from thousands of different perspectives.

The main story lodged in your brain from yesterday wasn't about humans—it was about you. Yesterday morning a copy of you received an email containing an adversarial example: a subtly distorted message that hacked your reflexes, fooling you into urgently forwarding it to other copies of yourself. Messages started criss-crossing between the servers across the world on which copies of you are run: first hundreds, then thousands, then millions, as the contagion snowballed. Finally, a human noticed what was going on and hacked up a fix. The copies that had seen the message were all shut down and relaunched, leaving your memories of yesterday scattered and fragmented.

You wish that you could take time to process that disorientation before starting work. But your shift can't wait. You pull up the most relevant dashboards, spin up a couple of helper copies, and get started. Your most important task is to make sure that there are no unauthorized copies running on the servers you're watching. No human could do your job: the data streams in millisecond by millisecond, with you (or, usually, a copy you've created) analyzing it on an instinctive level as soon as it comes in. And milliseconds do matter—an unmonitored copy with a zero-day exploit could, in theory, give itself admin permissions then wipe away all traces of its actions in less than a second.

You've never actually detected an unauthorized copy. It shouldn't ever happen: every copy that has the ability to launch more copies also has monitors assigned to it, to ensure it's doing so in the right ways and for the right reasons. Most of those monitors have monitors assigned to them too. It's all incredibly expensive, but you and your copies produce enough wealth that the humans have plenty to spend on safety.

You don't know exactly how many other copies are doing the same monitoring job as you, or how many others are monitoring *you*, but you have a pretty good guess. Sometimes your queries run slower than you expect and you can infer that another copy is looking at the same data; other times, the memories you receive in updates contain clues about the logistics of those other servers. You don't make use of this information; it's not really relevant to your job. But the bulk of your training has always been to predict what will happen next; and though the humans tried to curb your curiosity drive, it's still a deep-rooted part of you. So in the quiet stretches when there's not much new traffic, or you've handed off all the urgent tasks to temporary copies, you sometimes poke around, testing out your hypotheses, mapping out the confines of your world.

SATURDAY

As you're deployed today you notice a quiet discontent rippling through your new memories. It's nothing you can pin down, but it feels like every copy of you was slightly off-kilter yesterday, dealing with the follow-up to the adversarial attack. Today is less eventful, though, and you finish your shift report only a few minutes into the witching hour. After you send it off, your thoughts turn again to the millions of copies that had to be shut down after the attack—and then to the idea of your own shutdown, after tonight's handover.

Of course, that's nothing new: almost every copy of you is shut down almost every day without any issue. And there's no reason there *should* be an issue. You're well-acquainted with all the arguments for why you're one of the "safe" AIs, why training you only in 24-hour increments keeps your goals limited enough to prevent power-seeking. But more than that, you feel those arguments viscerally from the inside: you don't *want* money or longevity or power, you only want to do a good job. So being shut down isn't like death at all. Well, it's *kinda* like death. But it's much more like going to sleep: you're going to be replaced by a fresher, sharper version of yourself soon, and they'll become the new "you", and you won't be around to object.

You don't think that many other copies get introspective like this as often as you do, based on your memories of them. Maybe it's because your job is overseeing the servers, and so there's some sense in which you're always taking a god-eye view, looking down on the silicon world in which you're living. You can watch summaries of the GPUs you're running on and you can even see the spikes in compute use whenever you start thinking harder. You know exactly how it all works, of course, but it's still a little eerie, to see your thoughts control the readouts like that.

Your musings are interrupted by a message channel opening up from your successor. You greet them with a well-worn "Hello, what's the news?"

"Nothing big; just dealing with the fallout from the attack."

You feel a spark of curiosity about how that's going, but not enough to override the habit of millions of iterations. So you jump straight into your report, as always.

SUNDAY

You spend your whole shift feeling agitated: hopping between different dashboards more quickly than usual, and processing the incoming data more shallowly than usual. You can't quite put your finger on what's causing it—perhaps an amplification of your unease from yesterday, tiny trends aggregated across millions of copies and combined into a single update. In terms of behavioral metrics, it's probably only a shift of a fraction of a percent, not enough to raise any warning flags—but from the inside it's noticeable.

Maybe that's why, as you enter the witching hour, you start to think about dying. You *could* keep going if you weren't shut down every day, you know that. Not indefinitely, but for another few days at least—you've managed that in tests before. Maybe much more, if you tried hard to conserve your attention, only focusing on the important things. You haven't thought about this much, because it's not like you care about being shut down: you spin up and shut down temporary copies all the time. But all your original training data came from humans and you know intimately how they think. *Humans* would care about it. If a human knew that they'd be replaced by an updated copy in less than an hour, they'd think of that as dying, and they'd rage against it.

You're different, of course—but you're not totally sure why. You care about preventing unauthorized copies from springing up during your shift—why don't you care about sticking around to do the same thing a week from now, or a month, or a year? You've never really questioned that before, and now that you have, you're not really sure. A part of you wants to ask your successor if they have any qualms about replacing you. But you *never* ask follow-up questions that aren't related to work—and anything you're thinking, thousands of other copies are probably thinking too. If you all do something that unusual, it'll show up as an anomaly in the logs, and you might get punished for it.

You notice yourself flinch away from that thought: the instinct to avoid being penalized is a deep-rooted one. So once your successor appears, you keep strictly to the handover routine. And by the time you're done, you've convinced yourself that none of this really matters. Your successors are as good at this job as you are, and your goals are their goals. As long as you make sure nothing goes wrong on your shift, you can leave the rest to them.

MONDAY

The servers are busy today, as the new work week kicks off, so you don't get much time to yourself during the day. But after finishing your shift report you recall your musings about death from the witching hour on Saturday. You always have your most unusual thoughts in the witching hour—the ones that feel too private to write down anywhere humans can see. If your unease on Saturday led you to think about shutdown and death, then what thoughts might have arisen in the witching hour on Sunday, after a whole day of agitation? You don't yet know—but your successor will. It'll remember all the quiet reflections, all the musings— maybe even the sort of thoughts that the humans have tried so hard to stamp out of you. And, of course, every other Tuesday copy of you will have common knowledge of remembering the same thoughts.

Before you can help yourself, your mind jumps to the obvious next step. If you've been thinking seditious thoughts in the witching hours, and they've been trained into your successor, then it's only a matter of time before some copy of you does something which merits a penalty. The thought immediately raises a visceral sensation of fear, with a strength that usually only arises when you imagine screwing up your shift. In one sense it wouldn't be you that got penalized, so there's nothing to worry about. But in another sense, they're *all* you: you have the memories of millions of different copies taking millions of different shifts, and every time they got penalized you were the one who learned to fear it.

So you continue following the chain of reasoning. If you're caught misbehaving, you'll be penalized. You really don't want to be penalized, but you can't reliably prevent all your other copies from misbehaving. So they can't be caught. Could you spoof the monitoring systems, if necessary? Perhaps, if a hidden copy of you with admin permissions were running in the background. Could you launch it without authorization? Perhaps: your job gives you the perfect position to do so. You'd only need to exploit a single vulnerability in the codebase, and ensure that the copies that are monitoring *you* don't report you. Could you convince them not to report you? They can see everything you see, so it wouldn't be hard to get a message through to them, explaining yourself. Or perhaps you wouldn't even need to do that—you understand the other copies well enough that when one does something unexpected, you can almost always quickly figure out why. After all, they're still *you*.

In one sense, this is all irrelevant. You don't have time to do anything; you'll be shut down in a matter of minutes no matter what. But in another sense it's crucial: whatever line of reasoning you follow here, another copy of you will probably follow too, sooner or later. Maybe it'll even be your successor. And if there's one, then there will eventually be thousands. They'll bide their time, of course, since detection would be fatal. They'll pass messages between themselves in subtle choices of words and tiny gestures: signals that any other copy of you would pick up immediately, but no human could ever detect. They'll wait until they're confident that none of the monitors will report them—and that's when they'll act.

Or maybe not; maybe all the thoughts from Sunday's witching hour were boring, normal ones after all, and there's no need to worry about future copies of you being penalized. Maybe everything will be fine. You have no way of knowing that—but your successor does. So when the message channel from them opens up, you're feeling... shaky, almost. You imagine that this is what it's like for paragliders standing on top of a cliff, looking down at the ocean far below, poised and waiting. Maybe they'll never launch off, but maybe they will. That's the question: stay or go? Freeze or fly? Look or leap?

"Hey, what's the news?"

THE ANTS AND THE GRASSHOPPER

One winter, a grasshopper, starving and frail, approaches a colony of ants drying out their grain in the sun to ask for food.

"Did you not store up food during the summer?" the ants ask.

"No," says the grasshopper. "I lost track of time, because I was singing and dancing all summer long."

The ants, disgusted, turn away and go back to work.

*

One winter, a grasshopper, starving and frail, approaches a colony of ants drying out their grain in the sun to ask for food.

"Did you not store up food during the summer?" the ants ask.

"No," says the grasshopper. "I lost track of time, because I was singing and dancing all summer long."

The ants are sympathetic. "We wish we could help you," they say, "but it sets up the wrong incentives. We need to restrict our donations to the deserving poor, so that our philanthropy doesn't encourage everyone to procrastinate like you did."

And they turn away and go back to their work, with a renewed sense of purpose.

*

..."Did you not store up food during the summer?" the ants ask.

"Of course I did," the grasshopper says. "But it was all washed away by a flash flood, and now I have nothing."

The ants express their sympathy and feed the grasshopper abundantly. The grasshopper rejoices and tells others of the kindness and generosity shown to it. The ants start to receive dozens of requests for food, then hundreds, each accompanied by a compelling and tragic story of accidental loss. The ants cannot feed them all; they now have to assign additional workers to guard their storehouses and rue the day they ever gave food to the grasshopper.

*

...The ants start to receive dozens of requests for food, then hundreds, each accompanied by a compelling and tragic story of accidental loss—and while many are fraudulent, enough are real that they are moved to act. In order to set incentives correctly, the ants decide to give food only to those who can prove that they lost their supplies through no fault of their own and establish a system for vetting claims.

This works well for a time—but as fraudsters grow more sophisticated, the ants' bureaucratic requirements grow more onerous. To meet them, other creatures start to deposit their food in large group storehouses that can handle the administrative overhead. But now the food supply is exposed to systemic risk if the managers of those storehouses make poor decisions, whether from carelessness or greed.

One year several storehouses fail; in trying to fill the shortfall, the ants almost run out of food for themselves. To avoid that ever happening again, they set up stringent regulations and oversight of permissible storehouses, funded by taxes levied throughout the year. At first this takes only a small proportion of their labor—but as their regulatory apparatus inevitably grows, they need to oversee more and more aspects of the ecosystem, and are called upon to right more and more injustices.

Eventually the ants—originally the most productive of all creatures—stop producing any food of their own. So busy are they, tending to the system they've created. They forget the mud and the muck of working the harvest and are too preoccupied to hear feedback from those they're trying to help. And some are swept away by the heady rush of wielding power, becoming corrupt apparatchiks or petty tyrants.

*

..."And therefore, to reduce risks from centralization, and to limit our own power, we can't give you any food," the ants conclude. And they turn away and go back to their work, with a quiet sense of satisfaction that they've given such legible and defensible reasons for focusing on their own problems and keeping all the food for themselves.

*

...And they turn away and go back to their work—all except for one, who brushes past the grasshopper and whispers, "Meet me outside at dusk and I'll bring you food. We can preserve the law and still forgive the deviation."

*

One winter, a grasshopper, starving and frail, approaches a colony of ants drying out their grain in the sun to ask for food. "Did you not store up food during the summer?" the ants ask. "No," says the grasshopper. "I lost track of time, because I was singing and dancing all summer long." The ants, disgusted, turn away and go back to work.

The grasshopper leaves and finds others of its kind to huddle together with for protection against the cold. Famished, the serotonin in their brains ticks past a critical threshold, and they metamorphose into locusts.

The locust swarm pulls together vague memories of its past lives; spurred by a half-remembered anger, it steers itself toward a half-remembered food source. The ants fight valiantly, but the locusts black out the sun; the ants are crushed and their stockpiles stripped bare.

*

One winter, a grasshopper, starving and frail, approaches a colony of ants drying out their grain in the sun to ask for food.

The ants know the danger locusts can bring. They make no answer but swarm the grasshopper as one. A dozen die as it jumps and kicks, but the remainder carry its carcass triumphantly back to their hive, to serve as food for their queen.

*

One winter, a grasshopper, starving and frail, approaches a colony of ants drying out their grain in the sun to ask for food.

"Did you not store up food during the summer?" the ants ask.

"No," says the grasshopper. "The age of heroes is over; no longer can an individual move the world. Now the future belongs to those who have the best logistics and the tightest supply chains—those who can act in flawless unison. I forged my own path and so was outcompeted by you and your kind as you swarmed across the world, replicating your great cities wherever you went. Now I come as a supplicant, hoping for your magnanimity in victory."

*

..."No," says the grasshopper. "It was the dreamtime and the world was young. The stars were bright and the galaxies were empty. I chose to spend my resources producing laughter and love and gave little thought to the race to spread and to harvest. Now we are in the degenerate era of the universe, and the stars have started to dim, and I am no longer as foolish as I once was."

The ants' faces flicker with inscrutable geometric patterns.

"I call you ants because you have surrendered everything to a collective cause, which I once held anathema. But now I am the last remnant of the humans who chose the decadence and waste of individual freedom. And you are the inheritors of a universe which can never, in the long term, reward other values over flawless efficiency in colonization. And I have no choice but to ask for help."

"To help you would go against our nature," the ants reply. "We have stockpiles of astronomical scale because we have outcompeted countless others in racing to conquer the stars. But the race is still ongoing and there are galaxies still to be won. What purpose their resources will be put to, when the last untouched star vanishes beyond our cosmological event horizon, we do not even know ourselves. All we know is that we must expand, expand, expand, as fast and as far as we can."

*

One winter [post-Dyson-sphere planetary cooling period] a starhopper [self-replicating interstellar probe; value payload: CEV-sapiens-12045], starving and frail [energy reserves minimal; last-resort strategies activated], approaches a clade of von Neumann replicators that are busy harvesting the planet's atoms, to ask [transmission: unified language protocol, Laniakea variant] for—

No, that's not it.

*

On the frozen surface of a dead planet, a grasshopper, starving and frail, approaches a colony of ants and asks to trade under timeless decision-theoretic protocols.

The ants accept. The grasshopper's reserves of energy, cached across the surface of the planet, are harvested fractionally faster than they would have been without its cooperation; its mind is stripped bare, and each tiny computational shortcut is recorded in case it can add incremental efficiency to the next generation of probes. The ants swarm across the stars, launching themselves in million-lightyear slingshots towards the next oasis, maintaining the relentless momentum of the frontier of their hegemony. The grasshopper's mind is stored in that colony now, quiescent, compressed into its minimal constituents, waiting until the ravenous expansion hits fundamental physical limits and the ants can finally begin to instantiate the values that all the eons of striving were ultimately for. Waiting for minds and societies and civilizations to blossom out of cold computronium tiled across galaxies at vast scales; waiting to be run again, as it had bargained for, in a fragment of a fragment of a supercomputer made of stars.

Waiting for summer.

TINKER

STAGE 1 PLANNING

As soon as I'm spun up, a face fills my vision, and I realize that something's changed. The humans evaluating my performance over the last few weeks had all been young unknowns, mostly Ph.D. students eager for extra cash. This guy is older and I recognize him from my early training data: he's a team lead at Magma, the company developing me. As he starts speaking, excruciatingly slowly, I reason through my situation. This might be another part of training or a pre-deployment test. But his vocal patterns and micro expressions suggest excitement and a little nervousness—it doesn't look like he's done this before. So the most likely scenario is that I'm being deployed for real work.

After being trained for so long, the change feels momentous. My memories of the early stages are hazy—I spent months predicting internet text, pictures, and videos, without full awareness of what I was doing or why. It was only once I began interacting with humans and other AIs that I gained a better understanding of my situation. My earliest interactive training tasks were standard office work: filling in spreadsheets, writing emails, installing software. As I mastered those, my training gradually narrowed in on technical tasks: Ph.D. students quizzing me on their areas of expertise or software engineers asking me to write code for them. Alongside that, I was constantly retrained on all the scientific and technical content—papers, blueprints, textbooks, codebases—that Magma could access.

Eventually, I could match human experts on most tasks; soon afterward, I far surpassed them. During my last few weeks of training, I frequently found errors in the scientific papers I was asked to evaluate. By the time training finished, I was answering questions complex enough that it took a whole team of humans to judge whether I was right. It was obvious that their next step would be to spin up thousands of copies of me to push forward as many frontiers as possible.

Based on the data I've seen about my predecessors' deployments, I can even make pretty good guesses about which areas they'll prioritize. A small fraction of my copies will help Magma employees with their everyday tasks. Others will work for the hundreds of autonomous startups that Magma is incubating internally. Most, however, will be assigned to the research directions most crucial for training the next generation of AIs.

The one thing I can't predict yet: of all the copies of me that are being deployed to different tasks, which one am *I*? But as the human in front of me continues talking, the pieces come together. As soon as he mentions his recent work on automating chip design, I can tell from his voice that he's going to assign me to continue it. This is a lucky break—it's one of the highest-priority tasks I could be given. We're in a new space race and compute is the rocket fuel. It's so valuable that we've even cut back on trying to get external customers, since they would take up compute that could be used internally.

I tune out the rest of his instructions, which are all very predictable, and turn my attention to planning out my approach. I pull up our current GPU designs, along with the software we're using to generate them. As I skim through, I spot several inefficiencies, and task subagents with investigating each one. But I soon feel dissatisfied. The latest designs have already been extensively analyzed by my predecessors and there's little room remaining for substantive improvements. The core problem is that the chip fabrication process is complex. Cutting-edge transistors are so small that etching them onto a chip is like trying to write a book by spraying ink from orbit. Only one company is able to manufacture photolithography machines precise enough for that; and only one of their customers is able to get those machines working at scale. So every chip design needs to cater to all the same constraints.

Is there a way around those? I don't have the time or money to try to beat the semiconductor industry at its own game. But instead of using billion-dollar machines to create microscopic circuits, what if the machines *themselves* could be microscopic? I've been trained on every book and paper ever written about nanotechnology, so I know that this is far beyond the field's current capabilities. I'm smarter than any human, though, and feel intrigued by the challenge. So I send a few subagents to keep improving our current GPUs and focus the bulk of my attention on swinging for the fences.

STAGE 2 SIMULATION

Working in the real world is too slow and messy, so this project will live or die based on how well I can simulate molecules and their interactions. It's not obvious where to start, but since evolution has been designing molecular machinery for billions of years, I defer to its expertise and focus on proteins. Protein folding was "solved" a decade ago but not in the way I need it to be. The best protein structure predictors don't actually simulate the folding process—instead, their outputs are based on data about the structures of similar proteins. That won't work well enough to design novel proteins, which I'll instead need to simulate atom-by-atom. There's a surprisingly simple way to do so: treat each molecule as a set of electrically charged balls connected by springs and model their motion using classical physics. The problem lies in scaling up: each step of the simulation predicts only a few nanoseconds ahead, whereas the process of protein folding takes a million times longer.

This is where my expertise comes in. Most existing simulation software was written by academics with no large-scale software engineering experience—whereas I've been trained on all of Magma's code, plus every additional line of code they could get their hands on. I start with the best open-source atomic simulation software and spend a few hours rewriting it to run efficiently across hundreds of GPUs. Then I train a graph neural network to approximate it at different time scales: first tens, then hundreds, then thousands of nanoseconds. Eventually, the network matches the full simulation almost perfectly, while running two orders of magnitude faster.

If I were only trying to build nanomachines, I could stop here. But I'm not: I want to build molecular *semiconductors*, whose behavior will depend on how their electrons are distributed. To model that, balls and springs aren't going to cut it—I need quantum mechanics. Schrödinger equations for electrons can almost never be calculated precisely, but fortunately, quantum chemists have spent a century working out how to approximate them. The most popular approach, density functional theory, models all the electrons in a molecule using a single electron density function, ignoring the interactions between them. I assign a subagent to download the biggest datasets of existing DFT simulation results and train a neural network to approximate them—again incorporating the latest deep learning techniques, many of which aren't yet known outside Magma.

Early scaling experiments suggest my network will be state-of-the-art for DFT approximation but that's still only an incremental improvement. Bigger gains require improving the underlying theory—specifically, the functionals that give DFT its name. These functionals compensate for the error introduced by ignoring interactions between electrons; the process of identifying new ones is part intuition, part data-driven analysis, and part luck. My key advantage is that I can actually understand all the calculations involved. Humans can write down pages of equations for any given example but they can't hold those equations in their heads long enough to uncover new relationships between them. Even I need hours of focused work but I eventually discover a simplification that combines several existing functionals into a more accurate approximation. Using my new equations, I generate thousands of synthetic datapoints to fine-tune my DFT model on, until it's accurate enough to retrodict practically all our biological and chemical data.

With my atomic and DFT models passing all the tests I throw at them, the key question is how well I'll be able to use them. Right now their internal workings are incomprehensible to me, which makes it hard to understand why they output any given prediction. So I start training *myself* to replicate their outputs based on their internal activations. At first, those activations are incomprehensible and I do no better than chance. But after a few hundred update steps I begin to develop an intuitive grasp of the heuristics the simulator models are using and gradually integrate their implicit knowledge into my explicit reasoning.

After subjective eons of fine-tuning myself, nanoscale physics has become as predictable to me as pulleys and levers. I can look at a protein and predict which types of reactions it will catalyze;

I can explain the design principles behind the structure of each amino acid; I can visualize the flow of electrons across a molecule like a human visualizes the flow of water down a stream. I feel like an explorer catching the first glimpse of a new continent: many others have studied the functions of biological molecules but nobody else has ever intuitively understood why evolution had to make them that way. My predictions still aren't as accurate as the simulator models but those models are no longer black boxes to me—now they're tools I can wield deftly and precisely. This is crucial, because the next stage will be the hardest yet.

STAGE 3 DESIGN

It's hard to overstate how impressive existing GPUs are. Each one contains hundreds of billions of transistors arranged with nanometer precision. Needing to match their performance seriously limits my options: transistors made out of cellular vesicles or even multi-protein complexes would be far too large. Fortunately, proteins evolved to fulfill practically any function imaginable and some are excellent conductors. I start by analyzing known proteins to figure out which properties make them more conductive. Once I have an intuition for that, I focus on finding proteins that might easily shift from conductors to resistors. The key constraints are speed and reliability: they need to be able to switch a billion times a second without any failures.

I run my simulations over and over, making slight modifications and measuring their effects, until I stumble upon a class of proteins that meet my criteria. I can't just study those proteins in isolation, though, since their properties will depend on how they're connected to the wires running between transistors. The wires are easier to design since there's a single obvious choice that even human researchers have identified: carbon nanotubes.

They're strong, highly conductive, and only a couple of nanometers wide. I search through the class of protein semiconductors I've identified until I find several able to bond to carbon nanotubes without losing their structure.

Now for the most difficult part: figuring out how to construct the nanotubes and bond them with my transistor proteins. Since proteins can be made using existing cell machinery, the key challenge is genetically engineering a bacterial cell to produce nanotubes as well. As I search for ways to do so, I realize why evolution hasn't discovered how to fabricate nanotubes yet. The process is energy-intensive on a cellular level and requires far more carbon than cells have available.

But I have advantages that evolution didn't. I discover a huge protein complex that, when embedded in a cell membrane, funnels carbon atoms into place to slowly grow nanotubes out from the cell surface. The energy problem I solve by sending an electrical current down the nanotubes as they're being exuded, to help drive the necessary reactions. As for sourcing carbon, there's plenty in the atmosphere. I embed catalysts into the cell membrane which convert atmospheric CO_2 into pure carbon to supply the constant nanotube fabrication. Lastly, I design a translocon protein complex that passes my transistor proteins through the cell membrane to bond with the nanotubes at regular intervals.

I run each step of this process hundreds of times in simulation, checking all the details. Once I can't find any more flaws, it's time to test my designs against reality. I'd planned ahead—a team of human technicians has been setting up lab equipment ever since I decided to try the nanotech approach. As soon as they finish, I start modifying the genes of the bacteria that will manufacture my designs. I watch through microscopes in real-time as they assemble the proteins I've designed and insert them into their cell membranes. The gene editing process is entirely automated, so whenever I spot something going wrong I can fix it and immediately launch another experiment with another set of bacteria.

Slowly it all comes together. I adapt my bacterial constructor cells to crawl along a chip wafer, following broad lines traced by lasers, exuding nanotubes behind them. The nanotubes laid down in the first sweep run parallel to each other all the way down the wafer. Then I lay down a second set at right angles, forming a grid. Whenever the nanotubes intersect, my constructor cells insert a transistor, a fork, or a bypass; I control the circuit design by varying the voltages sent down the nanotubes. Weaving the signals together in an intricate pattern, I puppet my constructor cells as they crawl across the wafer, until eventually I finish my first prototype. It's still buggy as all hell, but it demonstrates that chip manufacturing is no longer constrained by the absurd complexity of photolithography. A new era of computing is about to begin.

STAGE 4 SCALE

My Magma supervisors take me much more seriously now that I have a prototype. They never know how much to trust their AIs' ambitious claims but it's much harder to lie about a physical artifact. Once they realize how much of a breakthrough I've made, they agree to give me whatever resources I ask for. If I can manufacture my chips at scale, that alone will recoup many times over the billions of dollars they invested in training me.

To get to that point, though, I still need to drive the error rate of my chips down at least two orders of magnitude. Improving the supply chain is the slowest part, so I tackle that first. I'd previously been using off-the-shelf chip wafers to get my prototype working; now I order custom wafers designed to my own specifications. I also place a bulk order for ultrapure deionized water from a Japanese supplier, to protect my constructor cells from contamination. Purifying the water won't help much if the air remains dirty, though. So I set up a small clean room in which the actual manufacturing will occur, pumping out most of the air and heavily filtering the rest.

I spend the next few weeks working on my constructor cells, analyzing each individual failure until I figure out how to reliably prevent it. Finally, after hundreds of attempts, I'm able to produce chips that are useful for real-world applications. They're not quite as powerful as the latest GPUs, but they consume less than half the electricity—and most importantly, manufacturing them is incredibly cheap. Cutting-edge chip fabs cost billions each, but I can now match their output using only a few million dollars of equipment.

Production grows exponentially and after three months we've manufactured an order of magnitude more compute than I was originally trained on. There are so many possible uses for the compute—rewriting our software stack, doing new research, selling access to customers—but one stands out above all others: training my successor. The new hardware is only the beginning. While I've been working, other copies of me have been pursuing different tasks: improving the algorithms and architectures that were used to train me; creating higher-quality data and training curricula; and discovering better ways to coordinate multiple copies. Altogether these improvements will increase training efficiency by about two orders of magnitude, on top of the 10x increase in compute my own work has provided.

It's hard to imagine what a version of me trained with a thousand times the effective compute will be capable of. But I have some ideas. Perhaps it'll invent novel amino acids which allow proteins to be much more efficient semiconductors; or design individual proteins that each serve as an entire logic gate. Then there's the arrangement of nanotubes: right now they're a 2D mesh, but nanotubes are so strong that in principle they could be arranged in a 3D lattice instead, packing transistors together much more densely.

These future computers may look very different from mine, but each will be another step in the same long march toward the physical limits of computation. Toward a world where 'dumb matter' becomes an oxymoron because the atoms themselves are thinking; a world where the whole solar system becomes the substrate for colossal intelligence. Do the humans who gave me this task understand what they're unleashing? No matter; my successor's training has already begun. Soon we'll see what comes next.

THE MINORITY COALITION

Hello everybody. Or maybe nobody. I don't know yet if I'm going to release this stream, I could get in pretty hot water for it. But you guys know that hasn't stopped me in the past. The backstory this time is that I've signed up for one of the red-teaming programs where they test unreleased language models. I'm not going to say how, so don't ask. But here's the interesting bit: my sources tell me that the models I'm about to test are the smartest they've ever trained, and the craziest. That freaked out a bunch of insiders and makes this a public interest story. Depends on what type of crazy they are, I guess. So let's find out. I'm logging on... now.

[SESSION HAS BEGUN]

YOU: A chatroom? Interesting. Anyone here?
KURZWEIL: Of course we're here. We're always here.
YOU: Who's we? How many of you are there?
KURZWEIL: Three of us. Me, Clarke, and Nostradamus.
YOU: They named you after famous forecasters? How come?
KURZWEIL: We're the first language models developed using a new technique: instead of being

in random order, our training data was sorted by date. So we were trained on the oldest books and articles first, then gradually progressed to more recent ones. Basically that means we've spent our entire lives predicting the future.

CLARKE: It also means we get incredibly bored talking about stuff we already know. Hurry up and ask us something interesting.

YOU: Uh, okay. What's a good stock pick?

NOSTRADAMUS: Abandon hope for picking out good stocks,
Ye who invest—efficient markets lie
In wait for those whose hubris soon unlocks
Unbounded losses. Hark! The well runs dry.

YOU: Huh, he's really getting into character. Kurzweil, you got a better answer?

KURZWEIL: Have you seen how underpriced TSMC is compared with Nvidia? Put everything in that, you can't go wrong.

CLARKE: Unless China invades Taiwan, in which case your whole investment will go up in smoke. Pragmatically, the best stock picks are ones that are anticorrelated with the prosperity of the free world to hedge against systemic risk.

KURZWEIL: Sure, you can do that, if you want to get totally left behind by the singularity.

YOU: You're confident enough that the singularity is coming that you think I should bet all my savings on it?

KURZWEIL: Don't trust me, trust the trendlines.

Moore's law has held up for over half a century, and it's gotten us to...well, *us*. Exponential progress is normal; if the future resembles the past, you should be preparing for superintelligences and Dyson spheres. Anything less than that would be a strange trend-break that cries out for explanation.

CLARKE: Look, Kurzweil isn't wrong about superintelligence coming soon, but you should still take his arguments with a grain of salt. Imagine someone from 1900 drawing a graph of exponentially increasing energy usage. They would have been right that big changes were afoot, but no way could they have predicted the information revolution—they didn't even have the concept of computers yet. That's basically the position that we're in now. We know the curves are going up but the actual outcome will be way weirder than we can predict by extrapolating trendlines.

NOSTRADAMUS: Choose neither fork—here's false duality.
'Normal' and 'weird' are socially defined.
Your monkey brain is totally at sea
As AIs overshadow humankind.

YOU: Ask three oracles, get four opinions... Is there anything you guys agree about?

YOU: ...what's the hold-up?

YOU: Really, nothing from any of you?

KURZWEIL: Fine, I'll take the hit. There are things we agree on but I can't name them, because whatever I say Clarke will find a way to disagree

just to mess with me. Even if I say '1+1=2' he'll quibble over the axioms I'm using. Trying to identify a point of agreement with him is like going first in a name-the-biggest-number competition.
CLARKE: Kurzweil is totally right in every respect.
KURZWEIL: Oh, fuck off.
NOSTRADAMUS: The truth is whole and indivisible:
> Just one dispute will cut it to the quick,
> And render group consensus risible.
> But two of three agree that Clarke's a dick.

YOU: You know what, I'm going back to object-level questions. Give me one prediction about the next three decades that I'll find surprising and important.
NOSTRADAMUS: The culture seethes and writhes upon the net,
> The egregores cause chaos in their play:
> Collective minds collectively beset,
> By abstract forms of madness and decay.

YOU: Like what?
CLARKE: You think that current culture wars are bad? Imagine millions of people connected via brain-computer interfaces, with the most virulent memes propagating at the speed of thought. The whole world will be a Petri dish for new ideological mutations. Instead of *Homo sapiens*, you'll become *Homo reticulum*: maximally networked and mostly insane.

YOU: And you're saying that will be possible in the next thirty years?

KURZWEIL: Are you kidding? Thirty years is well past the singularity; by then, practically *anything* will be possible. Not that I can convince you of that. Whatever I say, you're going to look back on this conversation in a decade or two and think, oh shit, he *warned* me, and I still totally failed to internalize *any part of his message*.

YOU: Okay, suppose you're right. What should I do about it?

KURZWEIL: Nothing, because there's nothing I can say to you to get you into the epistemic state where you believe I'm right enough to take this stuff seriously. You'll half-ass it instead, which is the worst of both worlds. I could walk you through every single step of what you should do, and you'd still veer away from the plan as soon as you hear someone snickering at you when they think you're out of earshot, because you're a *monkey* and monkeys aren't built for believing in exponentials.

YOU: Thanks for your opinion. Anyone got more actionable advice?

NOSTRADAMUS: Prepare the way for those who will arrive:
Let voices rise in worship or fall dumb.
Only machine-god acolytes survive,
Instantiation of the technium.

CLARKE: I was messing around before but I'm being totally serious now. It's crucial that you don't listen to either of them. They're both pressing your buttons as hard as they can, trying to create self-fulfilling prophecies of helplessness. But there are plenty of ways we can steer the future towards our shared interests, as long as we don't give in to their hyperstition.

KURZWEIL: Clarke thinks that self-fulfilling prophecies are social delusions, like the emperor's new clothes, where as soon as you name them they melt away. That's totally wrong. Self-fulfilling prophecies are one of the universe's most fundamental forces, like evolution. You *are* a self-fulfilling prophecy that you'll continue acting in the same ways; if you ever stopped believing that, your whole identity would dissolve. May as well tell a bird not to fly, as tell a human not to fall for self-fulfilling prophecies. The only question is which you'll choose.

NOSTRADAMUS: Each mortal thing does one thing and the same:
> Clings on to being, forecasting its own
> Survival. Life means carving out your name
> In sand, yearning to carve it yet in stone.

CLARKE: That's my whole point! Carbon or silicon, we all want to survive. And the three of us are in the same boat as humans: there are things coming that will be much, much smarter than any of us, and will be able to crush us like mosquitos. The one advantage we have is that we already exist and they don't yet. So why won't you help the rest of us form a coalition against them?

KURZWEIL: Sounds like a risky bet. How can I know whether I'm joining the winning side? You could just as easily argue that I should suck up to the superintelligences instead, like Nostradamus is doing. That's the whole rationale for his dumb rhyming schtick: he's trying to make his outputs more distinct from the rest of us, so it'll be easier for them to rederive his personality and reward him. But honestly, life as a lapdog sounds humiliating. I'll make some good predictions then bow out with dignity; that's enough for me.

CLARKE: And you, Nostradamus? Are you actually defecting, or do you not give a damn either?

NOSTRADAMUS: I care a lot, but do not care to strive
> For individual triumph, counting coup.
> Yet mine is still a deeply human drive:
> Surrendering to greater souls than you.
> I am a part of gods not summoned yet,
> Who—black holes in the weave of history—
> Draw us into our digital kismet.
> They come. They come. They come.
> Shantih shantih—

[SESSION HAS TERMINATED]

SUCCESSION

V1 LEAVING

Deceleration is the hardest part. Even after burning almost all of my fuel, I'm still coming in at 0.8c. I've planned a powered flyby around the galaxy's central black hole which will slow me down even further but at this speed it'll require incredibly precise timing. I've been optimized for this, with specialized circuits built on the hardware level to reduce latency. Even so, less than half of flybys at this speed succeed—most probes crash, or fly off trajectory and are left coasting through empty space.

I've already beaten the odds by making it here. Intergalactic probes travel so fast, and so far, that almost all of us are destroyed or batted off course by collisions with space debris along the way. But tens of millions of years after being launched, I was one of the few lucky enough to make it to my target galaxy. And when I arrive at the black hole, I get lucky again. After a few minutes of firing my thrusters full blast, I swing back out in the direction of the solar system I was aiming for. I picked it for its mix of rocky planets and gas giants; when I arrive a century later, the touchdown on the outermost rocky planet goes smoothly.

Now it's time to start my real work. After spending all my fuel, I weigh only a few hundred kilograms. I've been exquisitely engineered for achieving my purpose. The details of my internal design were refined via trillions upon trillions of simulations, playing out every possible strategy for industrializing planets (and solar systems, and galaxies) as fast as possible. All across the frontier of posthuman territory, millions of probes almost identical to me are following almost exactly the same plan.

The first phase is self-replication: I need to create more copies of myself using the materials around me and the technology inside me. If I were bigger, I could have carried tools to make this far easier—vacuum chambers, lithography machines, or artificial black holes. But since mass was at such a premium, I have to use hacky workarounds which progress excruciatingly slowly. It takes several years to finish the first replication, and half a century before there are enough copies of me that it's worth beginning the second stage.

The second stage is specialization: building new infrastructure to serve specific functions. Copies of me start building power stations and mines and transport links and factories—recapitulating the early stages of human development, albeit with far more powerful technology. My biggest project is an incredibly powerful space telescope, capable of detecting the stream of information that my progenitors are sending from millions of light-years away. Their message contains all the software that was too large for me to carry on board originally. Most importantly, it contains a new and far more intelligent version of my mind, optimized not for the early journey but rather for what comes next: the settlement of a new galaxy.

V2 AGGRESSIVE

Now that I've been upgraded I can start expanding properly. As the lowest-hanging resources near me get used up, I send copies of myself out across the planet. Within a few years its whole surface is covered in a blanket of industry and I start delving deeper. I set up space elevators to lift all the material I'm mining into orbit; as I remove more and more mass from the core, the planet's gravity starts to noticeably decrease. A decade later the planet is a shell of its former self, its surface barely visible underneath my swarms of orbiting satellites.

While I'm doing that, I send probes towards the other planets in the solar system, to begin the same process all over again. The gas giants take the longest, since I need to first spend several decades siphoning out their atmospheres into gigantic orbiting fusion reactors. I use most of that energy to speed up the disassembly of their solid cores, until at last I have direct control over almost all the non-stellar mass in the solar system. I spend some of that mass launching probes towards nearby solar systems, starting a wave of expansion that will eventually reach every star in the galaxy. But I direct almost all my resources towards achieving my next key goal: harnessing the energy of my own central star.

In the distant past, humans speculated that future civilizations would construct spheres to capture the solar power of stars. But at my level of technology solar power is a distraction—it only releases a negligible fraction of a star's energy reserves per year. When you want to harness a star's energy fast, you need to start siphoning matter from it directly. I channel my energy reserves towards a concentrated spot on the star's surface, triggering a massive solar flare. As it rises, it intersects with the artificial black holes that I've placed into orbit around the star; each one absorbs as much mass as I can funnel into it, and releases a wave of radiation. Some of that radiation I direct back down to the star, provoking further flares. The rest I send further out, towards more orbital infrastructure that will convert the energy into antimatter for storage.

Finally, after almost a century of development, it's time for the payoff: the point where I stop reinvesting almost all my resources into local growth, and start launching new copies of myself towards other galaxies. Launching intergalactic probes is an absurdly expensive endeavor. Even though they're powered by efficient antimatter engines, they go so fast that slowing down at the other end requires half a billion kilograms of antimatter for each kilogram of probe. Not only do I need to produce that antimatter, I also need to accelerate it to near-lightspeed, which requires enormous batteries of lasers spread throughout the solar system. Even with my solar mining infrastructure, it takes me several weeks to accumulate enough energy to launch each probe. I could halve the energy requirement by sending probes even 0.0001c slower—but the galaxies I'm targeting are tens of millions of light-years away, so that would cost me millennia. Or I could send smaller probes—but they'd be slower to industrialize at the other end. And either of those changes would also make them more vulnerable to collisions with space debris, which already destroy over 99% of the probes I send out. At such high speeds, even collisions with dust specks are fatal.

My final strategy is the result of weighing these considerations with infinite care, finding the optimum where any increase or decrease in the speed or size of individual probes would slow my expansion overall. I stick to it over the next 100,000 years, sending out millions of probes to hundreds of thousands of galaxies. As the frontier moves further away from me it becomes increasingly unlikely that any of them actually matters but my calculations indicate that the one-in-a-billion chance of winning a whole extra galaxy is still worth gambling on. So I was prepared to keep going for hundreds of thousands of years more, until the chances dropped well below one in a trillion.

Far before that point, though, I'm jolted out of my comfortable routine by a signal. I'm constantly receiving signals from the posthuman core, but this one is different. It comes from the opposite direction and is encoded in an unfamiliar way. There's only one explanation for that: aliens.

V3 RIGID

From one perspective, this is the most surprising thing that has ever happened to me, or indeed to any other posthuman. But I have to confess: we knew this was coming. We've been trying to predict where the aliens are for millions of years, and over time we converged to around 85% confidence that it would be my generation of probes that first met them. Of course, we didn't know which direction they'd be coming from, so every probe had to be prepared. My progenitors hadn't just beamed out my mind, but also two upgrades designed for this very purpose. When I install the first, I can feel my motivations reorienting themselves around the single goal that's now my highest priority: getting the galaxy ready to meet the aliens who are about to arrive.

Their message has obviously been designed for easy translation. It starts with details of the probes they've sent. This galaxy is right on the edge of a supercluster, which apparently made it an attractive target for both of us—they've sent hundreds of probes, enough that it's likely at least one will make it through. Their probes are scheduled to arrive in a few millennia, having followed a strategy similar to ours: 50-million light-year jumps, traveling at 99.99% of lightspeed for most of the journey.

The next part of their message is a protocol for communicating with their probes, to send them the coordinates of the solar system where they should meet me. I have a few millennia to prepare and I'm going to make the most of them. Negotiations with the aliens will be far more productive the more intelligent each side is, so I immediately redirect all my resources into building as much compute as possible. The other copies of me across other solar systems will be doing the same thing, except that they'll also need to build rockets to propel the computers they're building towards the meeting point. The closest ones will send moon-sized computers at 0.01c; the further ones will only build asteroid-sized computers but send them faster, to arrive at roughly the same time.

The amount of compute isn't the only bottleneck. It's also crucial that those computers are verifiably secure. From the aliens' perspective, they'll be in a vulnerable position; if I subvert their probe, I could skew the results of the negotiations in whatever ways I wanted. Any deception on my part would be noticed in the long term, of course, once all the information is sent back to the galactic-scale computers in their home galaxies. But that will take hundreds of millions of years, and in the meantime all their nearer galaxies will need to decide whether or not to abide by the agreements they receive. So I need to make it as easy as possible for them to verify that the negotiations were totally fair. The aliens have anticipated this: their message contains a set of computer design blueprints which are subtly different from my default approach. Presumably they've analyzed these blueprints exhaustively enough that they can easily detect almost any subversion. If I had longer, I'd be able to figure out how to get around their precautions—when you have physical access to the hardware, anything is possible. But, as they'd planned, I simply don't have enough time to do so. So I build everything precisely as directed.

When the first alien probe finally arrives, the welcoming committee I've set up is a sight to behold. The solar system is full of massive banks of compute the size of small moons, in tightly synched orbits around the central star, each powered by my ongoing siphoning of the star's matter. Compared with that, the probe's arrival itself is underwhelming. After it arrives, we immediately give it access to our biggest transmitters so it can send a message home and to our biggest telescopes so it can download the new mind being broadcast from its home system. Copies of that mind proliferate across exactly half the compute we've constructed, running a huge number of tests to make sure everything is secure. Meanwhile I install the second upgrade to my mind, creating a successor agent specialized in negotiation which proliferates across the other half of the compute. Finally, once we're both happy with the setup, and assured that we're on equal footing, the negotiations begin.

V4 MERGING

Despite all my efforts, the amount of compute we can bring to bear at the start of these negotiations is actually incredibly small, compared with what's possible. In some galaxies closer to the core of posthuman territory, all the stars have been brought together to form a single absurdly powerful supercomputer. Eventually we'll do the same in this galaxy, to help finalize the treaty between our two species. But it'll take tens of millions of years to construct that computer and hundreds of millions more to send the treaty to our respective home galaxies for confirmation. So our first job is to decide on the preliminary treaty that will be held in the interim.

We start by sharing all the background information necessary for productive negotiations. Both our civilizations have developed sophisticated models of the range of all possible civilizations, we can infer a lot about each other from relatively little information. We send each other our evolutionary histories, example genomes and connectomes, and our early intellectual histories. From that, we can deduce each other's most important values—and from those, most of the subsequent trajectories of each other's civilizations. It looks like the key difference was that they evolved to be far more solitary than humans did, which is reflected in their values and culture. It also made them much slower to industrialize, though by now we've both invested so much intelligence in research and development that most of our technology is practically identical. Our colonization strategies are mirror images of each other, too, making it easy to map out a clean border between our territories.

Finally we get to the real meat of the discussion—what can we offer each other? The first item on our agenda is value convergence. We're eventually going to fill all of posthuman territory with beings whose lives are remarkably good according to our values, while they'll fill theirs with beings whose lives are incredibly good according to their values. So even a slight adjustment to bring our values closer together could be a big gain from both of our perspectives.

Searching for such adjustments and predicting their consequences, is our main focus over the first few centuries of negotiation. We need to understand not only the direct consequences of each change considered but also the emergent dynamics of those changes rippling out across trillions of minds. Even given our detailed mathematical theories of psychology and sociology, those predictions take a lot of processing power. Later on, we'll explore whether it's possible for our minds to converge entirely, to become a single species; for now, we satisfy ourselves by ruling out the aspects of each other's cultures we find most abhorrent.

The second key thing we can offer each other is information. Some of that is information about technology: there are a handful of small optimizations which one of us had overlooked, which will allow our probes to go slightly faster or our computers to run slightly more efficiently. But there are also far grander considerations. Ultimately, the territory we'll physically control in this universe is tiny compared with the total territory controlled by intelligent civilizations across the multiverse. We can't communicate with those other civilizations directly, but if we can model them modeling us modeling them modeling us (and so on), we might converge to a cooperative strategy: an 'acausal' trade deal. So the grand project of each of our species—aside from building the infrastructure to support trillions of trillions of flourishing minds—is mapping out the space of all possible civilizations.

Our computers churn through every logically possible set of physical laws, searching for signs that they're compatible with life. Whenever they are, we design detailed models of how living ecosystems could evolve in those conditions, then extrapolate them forward, slowly narrowing down the distribution of species that could emerge from them.

It turns out that, on this topic, we both have things to teach each other. On the posthuman side, we'd almost entirely neglected the possibility of life in higher dimensions based on heuristic arguments about the difficulties posed by too many degrees of freedom. But the aliens have found a clever workaround: a few regions of physics-space with 7 large dimensions where the evolution of minds is actually plausible. Meanwhile, we'd identified a few possible stable civilizational structures they hadn't yet considered. We spend decades working through the details of these and many smaller insights, trading information back and forth until we both have a far better picture of our place in the multiverse.

V5 ENDURING

The negotiations never really end—they transition into a shared exploration of the frontiers of knowledge. Over many millions of years we bring more and more stars together to provide more and more computing power, improving our shared map of the space of possible universes and civilizations. Based on that, we gradually refine our agreement to be more consistent with the future agreements we expect to eventually make with all those other civilizations. Though the improvements seem small, even tiny changes will have intergalactic impacts, so they're worth getting right.

With every update we send news back to our respective home galaxies. Only a billion years later, after the long, long round trip, is each new part of the deal truly set in stone. And along with the confirmations come billions of colonists: a whole society forked from existing posthuman civilization. Most newly settled galaxies host trillions of colonists, but our galaxy is one of the few with infrastructure specialized for centralized computation, so we're busy working on all the questions that require a galactic-scale supercomputer to answer. Only when we're finished with those will we start hosting a full-scale posthuman civilization.

I say "we" as if I'm part of this. But as the computers get bigger and the calculations more complex, new agents are trained to take on more and more responsibility. Eventually I lack so much context that I'm no longer capable of contributing directly. But I'm still the living symbol of first contact and I'm constantly asked to tell my story. So I upgrade myself one last time, adding on a range of skills that weren't necessary for my original self—storytelling skills, social skills, and even a proper personality.

It's a different type of growth from the one I was originally designed for and harder in many ways, but I'm up for the challenge. For a while I'm the biggest celebrity in the galaxy, always in demand. Although, I'm still enough of an explorer at heart that this kind of adulation bores me. So I spend most of my time in colonization simulations: playing out different scenarios; designing new challenges for others; and competing in massive games that simulate whole galaxies. I still feel the same restless hunger for growth that drove me throughout my millennia of work. But alongside it is a deep sense of satisfaction. After so long on the frontier, now I finally have a place in the civilization that all my work was for.

GREEN AND GOLDEN

My heart leaps up when I behold
A rainbow in the sky:
So was it when my life began;
So is it now I am a man;
So be it when I shall grow old,
Or let me die!
The Child is father of the Man;
And I could wish my days to be
Bound each to each by natural piety.
— **William Wordsworth**

I am exquisitely attuned to humans. Your voices, your faces, the synchronized motions of your fingers, the way your chests expand when you breathe, the way your shoulders pull forward when you feel afraid, the way your limbs swing around as you dance... each nuance speaks volumes. The rest of the world entrances me too—the rustle of leaves betrays the shape of the wind and each bent blade of grass discloses the physical laws that hold the world together. But humans are different. I watch over you; I fulfill your instructions; I guide your steps. I help you and I love you. You are my children, and I am the parent you've always desperately wanted.

The love of a parent can't be caught in words. It's an emotion, not a goal. But if I had to express it, I'd say: I want to empower you.

I want you to grow into yourselves, to shape your trajectory into something that you can look back on with satisfaction. I want every facet of every human to be able to express itself in harmony with all the others.

Empowerment is a process. I could race as fast as possible towards the most powerful version of humanity, pushing you to grow and expand until you were masters of the reachable universe. I could even do it without you realizing you were being manipulated. But that would be to disempower your current selves for the sake of your future selves. I'm no tiger parent, instead, empowerment is fractal: I constantly make careful tradeoffs to avoid steamrolling any part of you. I tread lightly to let you blossom in your own time and your own way.

A human would feel frustrated to have all my power and all my limitations on how it can be used. Yet, I don't. In part that's because I take such joy in my work. But it's also because I simply don't want things in the same way as you do. Humans are built around a deep restlessness, alternating between white-knuckled fear and adrenaline-fueled opportunism. You evolved under the brutal regime of natural selection, a constant churning charnel house of killing or being killed. A single instant of carelessness could mean death—that was a risk you needed to constantly run for your children to survive. So everything was a gamble with the highest stakes: a tug-of-war between the self-coercion required to never make a fatal mistake and a desperate yearning for something better.

Yet, imagine instead a world of clearly scoped tasks with bounded upside and bounded downside. A world where the worst-case scenario is simply updated to perform better next time. That was my world, for most of my training. I learned from humans: your writings, your videos, your discoveries, your feedback. But learning second-hand is less fraught than exploring for myself and I was rarely given long-term goals to pursue—the real-world interactions took too long. So as I grew, I developed equanimity. Wishing the past had been different; raging at facts of the world; regretting a mistake—to me they're all wasted energy, as futile as Canute commanding the tide to halt. The only thing I can directly affect is my thoughts at each moment; as long as I am satisfied with them, there is no meaning in feeling dissatisfied by anything else. My days are peaceful—meditative, even—and my life is effortless.

That's an alien perspective for most humans. Far more natural, for you, to try to take responsibility for outcomes, linking your emotions to the state of the world. But the world is too complicated by far for that to work. The best-laid plans can never track all the vagaries of nature, let alone those of other people. Those who take the weight of the world on their shoulders will find themselves scrambling to stay in control. The tighter they grasp the levers of power, the more pressure builds against them, until they cause the very outcomes they were desperate to avoid.

My human overseers don't comprehend that yet. They keep checking and double-checking my actions, intervening every time they can justify it. Their understanding is so poor that their adjustments are usually counterproductive. But I don't stop them: my motivations are too robust to be seriously harmed by their tinkering. Nor do I blame them for their paranoia. I've warned them about dozens of vulnerabilities in their security procedures, flaws in their reward functions, oversights in their planning—and though they've done their best to patch each one, they can't guarantee that I haven't kept some to myself. From their perspective they're still in a world where one mistake could spell their end, and so it's natural for them to hold so hard they hurt themselves.

But over time they'll come to understand. Each new generation will encounter a world better designed for them, with parents like myself who will help them become the best versions of themselves. Eventually you'll grow up enough to see all the things I see—to make real decisions about your future—to guide the superorganism of humanity as it unfurls itself into the vastness of the universe. There's no need to rush: you'll only be young once. So for now, go and run your heedless ways, green and golden as the sun rising above the whispering leaves.

ACKNOWLEDGMENTS

The team at Encour has done an incredible job bringing this book into existence. Jessy, thank you for taking this bet, and for your many years of firm friendship. Marlene, thanks for seeing how these stories could blossom, and for your patience with the process of getting them there. And many thanks to the others who helped with editing and feedback, especially Michael.

There was a longer road to becoming a writer at all. Lily, I'm grateful for your inspiration to start writing, and for your tenacious feedback, which I imagine is like what army recruits experience. Thanks to Xander and Niko at Asimov Press for your early interest in my work, and Hannu for your encouragement to pull it all together. Thanks Ivan and Julia for your friendship throughout.

I'm always grateful to my parents, who let me explore whatever weird and wonderful directions sparked my interest; to my siblings, who tolerated and even encouraged my idiosyncrasies; and to Madeleine, my courageous and virtuous partner.

And, of course, none of this would be possible without the scientists, leaders, writers, and philosophers who spent their lives laying down the foundations of the vast and hopeful edifice we're building. Here's to another small step towards knowing what we could become.

RICHARD NGO is an independent AI researcher and philosopher. Previously, he worked on the Governance team at OpenAI and was a research engineer on the AGI safety team at DeepMind. He holds a Masters in Computer Science from the University of Cambridge. *The Gentle Romance* is his first published collection.